ZARA THORNE

◆

COMING HOME

D1353123

Complete and Unabridged

LINFORD
Leicester

First published in Great Britain in 2017

First Linford Edition
published 2019

*A catalogue record for this book is available
from the British Library.*

ISBN 978–1–4448–4168–8

Published by
F. A. Thorpe (Publishing)
Anstey, Leicestershire

Set by Words & Graphics Ltd.
Anstey, Leicestershire
Printed and bound in Great Britain by
T. J. International Ltd., Padstow, Cornwall

This book is printed on acid-free paper

1

Above the scuffed front door of the house, a string of bunting danced in the biting March wind. Holly Engleby could see the tips of the colourful triangles from her room on the first floor, the room she'd occupied throughout her first year at Birmingham University and one semester of her second.

She hadn't expected a goodbye party, hadn't even thought about it, but her housemates had thought otherwise, and last night the walls of the tall terraced house had become almost convex with the sheer number of people packed inside. It had come as a shock, in a good way, that so many had bothered to come. But any excuse for a party. All the same, she'd felt flattered, and because there was such a crowd, nobody had noticed she wasn't drinking. Bethany had put a glass in her hand containing fizzy water with ice and a wedge of lemon. It looked like a posh vodka. Only her housemates — the female ones — and two other close friends knew why she was leaving, and they were sworn to secrecy. The official line was that she was disillusioned with her English Lit course and was taking time out to decide where she was heading next.

There was a perfunctory tap on the door and Bethany came in. 'You okay, Holls?'

'I think so.' Holly turned away from the window to smile at Bethany. 'I'm fine. I will miss this, though. The house, you, everyone.'

'Oh, don't!' Bethany rushed over and threw her arms around Holly. 'I'm gonna miss you like crazy. It won't be the same without you.'

'It's not as if we're never going to see each other again,' Holly said when Bethany released her. 'You can come and visit me at home, and we can share a house again if . . . *when* I come back.'

'Oh yeah, and exactly how's that meant to happen?' Bethany tossed her head, making her wayward dark curls rise then settle back around her shoulders.

Holly let a beat of silence fall before she said quietly, 'I don't know, Beth. I just know it has to be possible, that's all. I can't think that this is the end of this phase of my life.' She gave a little laugh. 'I won't be any use to anyone with only half a degree, will I?'

'But . . . ' Bethany looked doubtful and confused. But not as confused as Holly was.

Just get yourself back here, Mum had said, in the same voice she used when Holly was due home for Christmas. *Come back to Spindlewood and we'll sort it all out, together.*

Like it was ever going to be that easy. Mum knew that, of course. But she was right; it was no use closing her eyes and pretending it wasn't happening. Once she was back in Sussex, she'd be able to see things a lot clearer.

'Beth, would you do me a favour and take these books back to the library for me? I know it's unlikely, but I don't want to bump into anyone I know.'

'Would that *anyone* be called Lorcan Jones, by chance?'

Holly sighed. 'I passed him in town the other day and he only waved at me from across the road. It's not worth the risk, though. I can do without the complication.'

'If he catches on that you're leaving, he might do more than wave.'

'Exactly. My luck's held so far. I don't want it running out now.'

Bethany's eyes flicked towards Holly's middle. 'I wouldn't exactly say your luck's held.'

The two girls laughed. It felt like old times. *Old times*, already!

'Seriously, though,' Bethany said, 'are you really not going to have that conversation with Lorcan?' She drew air-quotes around 'that conversation'.

Holly half-turned towards the window.

'You're making rather a big assumption, Beth.'

'So if it wasn't Lorcan, then . . . Okay, sorry. It's your business. As long as you're all right, that's all I care about.'

Holly turned back and smiled. 'I will be, don't worry, but I need to be out of here. My train's at two.' The train wasn't the only reason she didn't want to delay this any longer than necessary. She'd held it together for this long; it wouldn't do any good to spoil it now.

'Station?'

'Amber's giving me a lift.'

'Want me to come?'

'Do you mind not?'

'Nope, it's cool.' Bethany smiled.

Holly peered down into the street, willing Amber's white Mini to appear. It didn't, but she'd be here soon. Everyone was being so good to her, so cool about everything. She would never forget that, whatever the future held.

Tears threatened. She smothered

them. 'I've still got a few bits to pack.'
She nodded towards her already bulging rucksack. 'Stuff from the bathroom
and that.'

Bethany picked up the library books
and made for the door, understanding
Holly's need for a moment to herself.

'Don't forget to say goodbye before
you go.'

'Course not.'

2

Holly stood beside the public footpath sign at the top of Charnley Hill. She shaded her eyes with a gloved hand against the acid-bright sunshine to gaze at the panoramic view of fields, winding lanes, and the South Downs, smudgy beneath a gauze of mist, in the distance. To her left, the fringes of Charnley Acre were just visible, the rest of the village hidden by the woods. Was it really only three months since she was last here, home for the Christmas vacation? It felt like several lifetimes.

On the way up the hill, she'd seen powdery tassels of catkins bursting with pollen, clusters of star-shaped white anemones lighting the woods, and tight green buds ready to break. Signs of spring, but more than that; all this new growth, new life, seemed heavy with special significance.

Holly opened the gate and stepped onto the footpath which led down the hill, following the line of the woods. Being so early in the day, it was perishing cold, and the grass on the shady side of the path was rimed with silver; but in a strange way she welcomed the loss of feeling in her toes and the sting of the air on her face. She should probably have had breakfast before she came out, but since she'd arrived home the day before yesterday, she'd felt increasingly restless and unable to settle to anything, let alone stay indoors. Yesterday she'd spent most of the morning wandering around the garden, and in the afternoon she'd walked down to the village.

Mum was being brilliant as usual, letting her do whatever she wanted, at whatever time. Not asking to keep her company, or forcing meals on her, or suggesting bed-times, or any of those things that came naturally to her as a mother, and Holly was grateful for that.

The trouble was, this easy-going

attitude was only adding to the guilt that Holly felt about her mother. The disappointment, the worry, the fear for Holly's future; it was all there, in Laura's eyes. It was up to Holly to try and make this as painless as possible for her mum, although quite how she was going to manage that was anyone's guess.

'I've let you down, Mum,' had been Holly's first words when she'd walked in the door of Spindlewood. 'And Dad, too. He'd have hated this.'

Laura had said nothing. She'd simply opened her arms for Holly to walk into, and for a warm, delightful moment, Holly could believe that everything was normal and ordinary and safe. It wasn't until later that evening, when they'd been sitting at the kitchen table after a quiet, thoughtful dinner, that Mum had set down her glass of water and said, 'Now tell me it all, Holly. In your own time.'

All. Understandably, Mum had wanted truth and detail, not a carefully curated account.

'I never meant it to happen,' she'd begun.

'Obviously.'

'I took the morning-after pill, but it failed. I was stupid. I made a mammoth mistake. You don't need me to go into — '

'No, no.' Mum had held up a hand. 'I get that, of course I do, but just tell me this. When you were home at Christmas, you didn't say you were seeing anyone. So, are you now?'

'No. I wasn't then, and I haven't been since.'

Mum had nodded. Having had it confirmed there was no regular boyfriend on the scene, to Laura's credit she hadn't asked who, or how, or why, or any of the other obvious questions. Other mothers would have, Holly was aware of that, and those questions might come eventually. If they did, she'd deal with them then. But for now, uppermost in Mum's mind was how Holly felt about what had happened, and what she wanted to do about it. The trouble was, she didn't know.

Except for one thing. Trying not to notice her mother's flinch and the rapid movements of her chest, she'd told her about the visit to the clinic — one in town, nowhere near campus — where she'd talked through the termination process with the counsellor. It was what her friends had expected her to do — Bethany, Ruomi, Amber and Erin. Explore the options, as it said on the none-too-discreet posters in the toilets at uni. It was what she'd expected herself to do. And so she did it, while deep down she'd known she was ticking a box, nothing more.

She'd come out of the clinic and dropped the information pack straight into the nearest litter bin before linking arms with Bethany and Ruomi, who'd been waiting for her on the corner. Then they'd gone to the Bullring for hot chocolate.

Mum had smiled when Holly reached this part of the story, a smile that was a little bit sad and a little bit crooked. Holly felt she should have cried at that point. If she'd been writing the script, the tears would have flowed, no danger. But it hadn't happened. She'd remained dry-eyed, as she had right from the start.

Her stomach was beginning to complain about the lack of food, and she increased her pace on the footpath. At the bottom of the woods, the path branched out, leading across the middle of a field to the right, and past the woods on the left where it would emerge at the crossroads at the bottom of Charnley Hill. She took the left-hand fork. On the lower ground, the path became sticky underfoot where moisture had gathered in the ruts and turned the earth to clay that stuck to her boots. Perhaps it would have been better if she'd turned round and gone back the way she'd come. Too late now. Her mind didn't seem to be up to making basic decisions of that kind, as if all the relevant brain cells were busily engaged elsewhere.

At the end of the footpath, she gave her boots a wipe on the long grass by the fence-post, then began the trek up Charnley Hill. Spindlewood looked as welcoming as ever, with its twinkling windows looking out from rosy brickwork, its storybook chimneys, and the quirky turret wearing a gnome's-cap roof. They'd lived here like forever, the three of them. And then, when she was just fourteen and Mum only forty, Dad — her dearest, lovely dad — had got cancer, and in the end there was nothing anyone could do.

'I'm so sorry, Dad,' Holly whispered to the sky as she made her way up the drive towards the house. 'Your idiot daughter messed up big time. I'm sorry.'

'There you are.' Laura was coming towards her, her unbuttoned coat flapping open. 'I was coming to look for you. You shouldn't have gone out without breakfast, and it's so nippy out here. Come on in before you catch your death.'

She took Holly's arm and almost frogmarched her up to the house, round to the back door and into the warm fug of the kitchen. So much for Mum being cool and letting her do her own thing.

'I'm fine, Mum.'

Holly shrugged out of her coat and dropped into a chair. She hadn't realised how tired she was, and how much the walk had taken out of her. At least she didn't have morning sickness to contend with. That had come as a surprise, but apparently not everyone got it.

'Ooh, you made pancakes.' The pan was on the stove, four golden pancakes on a plate beside it.

'I did, but they'll have gone cold now.'

'Sorry. I just needed some air. I'll tell you next time.'

'It's okay, love. I'll try not to be overprotective, but I can't guarantee I'll be able to keep it up. Shall I nuke these for you?' Laura had the plate of pancakes in her hand.

'I'll do it,' Holly said, half getting up.

'No, sit still.' The plate made its way into the microwave; a dish of blueberries and the squeezy bottle of maple syrup arrived on the table, along with a mug of tea.

The sight of the syrup almost made her gag. So much for getting away with the sickness thing. 'Just the blueberries, I think.'

'You'll find you go off certain foods. I did. It's all perfectly natural.' Laura sat down opposite Holly, watching her tuck into her overdue breakfast. 'Sorry, Holly. The last thing you need is me forcing information down your throat, as it were.' She gave a little laugh.

Holly sensed something more to come. Obviously her mother had things on her mind. She was right.

'I have to ask this once, but it will only be the once. Holly, are you totally sure you don't want to end the pregnancy? I know you don't believe in abortion, but principles can change once it becomes personal and there's nothing wrong with that.'

'I am sure, Mum. Absolutely.'

'Then I accept what you say, and I shan't mention it again.' Her mother began pushing her empty tea mug slowly around the table with one finger, as if she was using a ouija board, then stilled the mug. 'So, then. Your twelve-week scan. Would you say it's due around the end of the month?'

In other words, when exactly did this 'mistake' happen?

Laura was the best mum anyone could wish for. They'd always been close, the two of them, even more so since Dad died. Even so, a certain amount of information editing was necessary in some situations. Holly finished her last pancake before she answered. She hadn't realised how famished she'd been.

'Around then, yes.'

'Right, we must get you booked in.'

Laura's expression was one of bright efficiency.

'I'll do it.'

'Yes, of course. You do it. Just ring the medical centre and — '

'I know.'

'Of course you do.'

'I'm so sorry to bring all this on you,' Holly said. 'You don't deserve it.'

Laura stood up from the table and picked up Holly's plate. There was one blueberry left on it. She popped it into her mouth. 'Holly, please stop apologising. You're my daughter and I love you. I'd do anything to make you happy if it was in my power, you know that.'

'Yes.' Holly nodded, feeling suddenly emotional.

'Does he know?' Laura looked startled, as if her own question had made its way out of her mouth of its own volition.

'No. He's not part of this.' Holly heard the unintentional vehemence in her voice.

A plate clonked against the side of

the sink. 'But he *is*, Holly. For goodness sake, it takes two to make a baby!'

'*Mum* . . .'

'Well, I'm sorry, but you need to tell him. You don't have to tell me who it is — not if you don't want to — but he has to be put in the picture. You think you know what you want now, but you may regret it in the future if you go down that route.'

Her mother's face had turned pink. Again, Holly felt sorry for her. Laura didn't want this any more than she did herself. But it wasn't up for discussion. Not now. Not ever. She stood up from the table.

'I won't be swayed, Mum. This is what's right for me and right for the . . . for everyone, and I'm sorry but I really don't want to talk about it.'

Laura subsided against the sink, her hands heeled on its rim. She looked defeated, and suddenly older than her forty-seven years. But Holly had to stay strong; she had no choice. She went across and put her arms around her mother, feeling her stiffen beneath her touch.

Upstairs in her bedroom, Holly lay face-up on her bed, closed her eyes and tried not to think. After a few minutes she began to feel hazy, as if she could drop off to sleep. A little nap might be the best thing, considering her early start. The sound of a vehicle coming up the drive and rumbling to a stop disturbed her. Holly rolled off the bed, went to the window and looked down.

The bright green van, with *Green and Fragrant Gardening Services* in orange lettering on the side, was parked in front of the house. It was here so often it was practically part of the scenery, as was its driver, Clayton Masters, Mum's boyfriend. Clayton glanced up at the window as he jumped down from the van. Holly waved, and Clayton raised a hand back before disappearing out of sight. She heard the front door open and close, and voices, indistinct, rising from below.

They were properly loved-up, those

two. It could be a bit embarrassing, thinking about your mother being in love. And as for what went with it, well, you hoped you would never, *ever* have to think about that. But Holly couldn't be anything but happy for Mum, especially after her previous relationship — her only other serious one since Dad — had ended disastrously. Mum and Clayton had been together, in an unofficial, low-key kind of way, since the Christmas before last. Then, as the months passed, they'd stopped pretending it wasn't serious, to each other as well as to the outside world, and become a proper item.

Clayton was so good for Mum; Holly had always thought so. There wasn't any sort of side to him, nothing you could tag onto and think, hey, what's that all about then? This attribute, she had now learned, was less common in men than you'd like it to be. Clayton was good-looking as well, which was always the cherry on the cake. Holly giggled.

It had gone quiet below. Perhaps Mum and Clayton were feverishly embracing in the kitchen. Well, too bad. The pancakes had only dented her appetite. Now she craved toast, with lots of butter.

On her way downstairs, Holly realised the kitchen door was open and she could hear the voices quite clearly. Her name was mentioned, twice. She sat down at the twist in the staircase, where one part led up to the circular room in the turret. This particular stair had been her special listening place when she was a child. The voices were low and serious, and yes, as she'd thought, Mum was telling Clayton about her being pregnant. Hearing the news being passed on — odd words of it, anyway — added a new dimension to her situation, a new reality, which sent little anxiety shocks up her spine. To be fair, though, Mum had asked Holly if she could tell Clayton and she'd agreed. She liked Clayton and trusted him to keep her secret. She had no problem with him knowing the real reason she'd come home, and besides, she couldn't expect Mum to lie to him.

The other person who was in on this was her mother's best friend, Emily. She was almost a member of the family, anyway, and Holly was glad she knew. Mum needed someone to talk to, and they'd agreed they wouldn't tell Gran, not until — unless — she needed to know. The same went for Mum's sister, Rachael. Neither she nor Gran lived nearby, and Mum didn't seem that anxious to share the news with them anyway.

As for other people, well, it was nobody else's business, was it? It was such early days yet, and she'd hardly had time to get her head around it herself. Some of her oldest friends, those who lived in Charnley Acre, would have to know, but again, not until Holly chose to tell them.

If it turned out that she needed to.

Continuing on down the stairs to the hall, Holly made a move towards the kitchen, but really, she would rather not face Clayton just yet. She didn't think she'd feel embarrassed — it wasn't as if she was ashamed or anything — but he might not know how to *be* with her, what to say, and she would hate to put him in that situation. Best to let the information sink in first.

Holly darted lightly back upstairs to her room. She changed her jumper for a warmer one with a polo-neck, grabbed her purse, and tiptoed back down to the hall. Hitching her coat from the hook and putting it on, she slipped quietly out of the front door. As she walked down the drive, she sent Mum a text: *Gone to the village. Won't be long. Text me if you need anything from the shops. H xx*

* * *

It would be sensible, and would please her mother, if she called in at Charnley Acre Medical Centre and made her appointment. It was past the end of the high street, where the shops petered out, set back from the road. She could walk along there now and get it over and done with.

She crossed the road to be on the same side as the medical centre, but as she did, she visualised the forecourt full of cars and the double glass doors opening and closing, letting a steady stream of patients in and out. This was Charnley Acre. The odds of there being somebody she knew — or who knew her — sitting in the waiting room, were sky-high. And it wasn't easy to keep your voice down when you were at the glass partition shielding the receptionists. She would phone instead, later today. Or tomorrow.

Holly continued her walk, stopping to look in the windows of the shops, taking pleasure in the familiar. Disregarding the reason, it was good to be back in the village. She'd have come home in a few weeks' time for Easter, in any case. It was late this year, but perhaps anyone spotting her in the village would think the university vacation had already started. She didn't want to care what anyone thought, she really didn't, yet it was hard not to. They'd all know anyway, once she started showing. Hopefully, that wouldn't be for ages.

Meanwhile, there were plans to be made. She couldn't just drift about at home and expect Mum to keep her. They hadn't had that conversation yet, the one where Mum asked her what she intended to do with herself for the next few months, but it would come. Besides, she'd be bored silly doing nothing. Already she was missing the rush to get to lectures on time, the dash across campus to hand in coursework assignments before the deadline, and the company, of course.

She was trying not to wonder constantly what Bethany and the others were doing at that moment, but it wasn't easy. They'd texted a few times. She and Beth and Amber had wanted to know if Holly had arrived home safely. They were still there, the girls, caring about her and always pleased to hear from her, but they were busy with their own lives; she mustn't expect too much from them. Her life was here now, in Charnley Acre, at least in the short term, and it was up to her to make the best of it.

Holly crossed the road again, just as the door of The Ginger Cat opened and someone came out. The aroma of coffee and baking that greeted her sent mixed signals to her brain; mouth-watering hunger fighting with faint nausea. Remembering the toast she'd missed earlier, hunger won. Holly went in and sat at a table at the back of the café. Lloyd, who ran The Ginger Cat with his wife, Jo, waved across as he noticed her.

'Holly! You're soon back. They don't keep you at it for long, these universities, do they?' He grinned.

'Nope.' Holly grinned back. Her heart beat a tiny bit faster. But this was what it was going to be like, and she'd better get used to it.

'As long as you're getting your money's worth. Bad enough in my time, trying to stretch out the grant till the end of term, but now . . . ' He made a whistling sound.

'Tell me about it,' Holly said.

'Be with you in a tick.' Lloyd turned his attention back to a customer who was waiting at the counter to pay.

Holly sat back in her seat and looked around. The familiar décor — cats on the walls, cats on the shelves, cats on the crockery — always made her smile. Even the pot plants arranged along the deep windowsills had tiny model cats on wires stuck into the soil. Jo jokingly referred to herself as the original crazy cat lady. She and Lloyd had at least two rescue cats at any one time in their Victorian terrace house by the park.

Jo didn't seem to be about this morning. Instead, a girl about Holly's age was waiting at table. From her sideways-on view, the tall girl with the athletic figure looked familiar, but

Holly couldn't quite place her.

Moments later, she was at Holly's table, dropping the menu into her hand. 'Ooh, I know you, don't I? You were in my class at Charnley Juniors.'

Holly's vague recollection of this smiling girl morphed into actuality. 'Oh, yes, it's Carys, isn't it? Carys Williams?'

'Yep. And you're Holly Engleby, right?'

'Right.' Holly smiled up at her. 'You had a lot more hair in those days.'

Carys had been famous in their little village school for wearing her dark brown hair so long she could sit on it. Now she wore it in a sharply cut inverted bob, its side flicks framing her attractive, strong-featured face.

Carys's laugh rang out across the café. 'I did. I got fed up with all that brushing in the end, and it wasn't very practical for swimming.' She nodded towards Holly's straight, pale blonde hair, the same shade as Mum's. 'Yours is still long. Looks gorgeous.'

'Thanks.' Carys had been famous for her swimming prowess, too, Holly remembered. 'You won the swimming sports cup in our last year of juniors.'

Carys affected a snooty air. 'My dear girl, I won *all* the cups, juniors and seniors.'

Holly thought for a moment. 'I don't remember you at senior school. I went to an all-girls, though. My parents' idea.' She raised her eyes. 'I expect you went to the other one, and I bet it was a lot more fun.'

'No, we moved away when I was eleven, to Wales, where Dad came from originally. He and Mum opened a small hotel in a little place on the coast, just outside Swansea. I only came back last year. How about you? Have you been away and come back, like me?'

'Something like that. It's a bit complicated.'

'Isn't it always?' Carys glanced behind her as the café door opened, and two couples made their way to the window tables. 'I'd better get on. Nice to see you, though. Let's have a proper catch-up soon.'

'I'd like that,' Holly said.

'Oh, what did you want?' Carys nodded at the menu Holly was holding. 'Some waitress I am!'

'Tea, please, and a round of fruit toast. No, make that two rounds. With extra butter.'

'Builder's tea? That's English Breakfast to you. We've got other sorts.'

'Builder's is fine.'

★　★　★

The fruit toast had been just what she needed. Holly gazed at the cats dancing round the rim of her empty plate and hoped she wasn't going to be this hungry all the time, otherwise it wouldn't only be baby weight she'd be displaying.

Oh. While she'd been talking to Carys and then enjoying her second breakfast, she'd pushed all that to the back of her mind. Now it surged forwards uninvited, sending her spirits into freefall. Holly sighed. She'd brought this on herself. Nobody had forced her to . . . she stood up and went to the counter to pay before the next in a long line of logical thoughts took hold.

Carys was working the coffee machine while Lloyd took her money. 'Holly! Come in again soon and we'll sort out that catch-up. A couple of drinks in The Goose and Feather maybe?'

Holly nodded. Was this wise, making new connections with people she'd have to explain everything to before long? And The Goose could be tricky. Being virtually the only night-spot in the village, it was the first place Holly usually headed for to catch up with the Charnley Acre crowd when she was home. She wasn't sure she was ready to run into any of them just yet, and there was the potentially embarrassing complication of the no-drinking thing. But she couldn't worry about everything.

Carys was like a breath of fresh air, and hiding herself away up at Spindlewood was definitely not part of her plans, whatever they turned out to be.

As she tucked her purse away inside her shoulder bag, she spotted a typed notice propped against a pot of honey on the counter. *Staff wanted. Speak to Lloyd or Jo.*

'Lloyd?'

'Yes, Holly?' Lloyd looked up from the tray of cheese scones he was decanting onto small plates.

She pointed at the notice. 'Would you take me on? I've got experience of dealing with customers from my supermarket job in Birmingham, but that's all, I'm afraid.'

'That's not a problem, but I'm looking for someone to work straight through till the end of summer, minimum. It's not a holiday job as such.'

Holly leaned into the counter. 'To tell the truth, I'm not going back to university, not for a while anyway. It's like you said. It costs megabucks, and I'm not enjoying my English course that much.'

The lies spilled out so easily, as if she'd already got used to telling them. It wasn't a good feeling.

Lloyd's face brightened. 'Well, in that case, you're on. Pop back tomorrow with your documents and I'll sort you out some shifts.'

3

Her twelve-week scan was over. Mum
had driven her to the hospital at
Cliffhaven and had come into the room
with her without making a song and
dance about it. Holly had wondered if
she would automatically experience a
rush of maternal feeling when the
image came on screen, but she'd felt
nothing except a short, sharp twinge of
anxiety, and then it was gone.

She had only glanced at the screen
for a few seconds. It was enough to be
told that everything was as it should
be; that was the only reason she was
here. She'd sensed rather than seen a
look exchanged between Mum and the
sonographer — her own gaze had
moved swiftly to the square of blue
sky framed by the window and stayed
there — but nobody tried to make her
look at the image for longer. If they'd

expected her to do or say anything other than 'thank you' at the end, they weren't showing it.

When she was asked if she wanted a print of the scan to take away with her, she'd shaken her head at the same as Mum had nodded. The picture had been passed quietly to her mother, who had slipped it into her bag, and Holly hadn't seen it since.

There had been one difficult moment on the drive home from the hospital when Mum had bitten her bottom lip and looked close to tears. As Holly was about to ask her what was wrong — as if she didn't know — Mum's expression had cleared, and she'd patted Holly on the knee and smiled then said, 'Well, that's done, then.'

'Yep, all done,' Holly had answered, because she couldn't think of anything else to say that wouldn't trigger the kind of conversation she couldn't handle.

As they'd passed through a village, Mum had suggested stopping off for hot chocolate.

'Aren't you due back at school?' Holly had said.

She was already feeling guilty about Mum having to arrange cover for her class. The school where she taught was for children with special educational needs. Those kids needed her mother more than she did.

'Nope. I rang earlier and arranged to have the whole day. I thought we could do something — a bit of retail therapy, perhaps. Or anything you like.'

'Actually, could we please just go home? Sorry.'

'Fine by me.' Mum had smiled and put her foot down.

Now, here they were, back at Spindlewood. Mum was upstairs somewhere, probably in the circular turret room where she went when she wanted a quiet think. She was doing a lot of that these days, which wasn't a surprise. It was also another reason to feel guilty.

Holly was in the kitchen, making gingerbread. Watching the butter, syrup, and sugar slowly melt into golden smoothness as she stirred was having a calming effect. She hadn't realised how tense she'd been since the scan. She'd been an idiot, thinking she'd managed to detach herself from what was happening. But as long as she kept a tight lid on any random thoughts and feelings that might escape, she'd be fine.

She'd just poured the mixture into the flour and the tins were in the oven when her phoned beeped. Wiping her hands on the dishcloth, she picked it up. It was Carys, ringing from The Ginger Cat. Holly could hear voices and the tinkle of china in the background.

'Holly, it's me. We never did go for that drink. How are you fixed for tonight?' Then before Holly could answer, 'Oh go on, say yes. If I have to watch one more episode of *Emmerdale* with Nan, I'll go stir crazy.'

'Yes, then,' Holly heard herself say.

So far, she'd only been out in the evening to go the cinema in Cliffhaven with Mum and Emily, and for pizza in Lewes with Mum and Clayton. The idea of going to The Goose and Feather and bumping into God-knew-who sent quivers down her spine, but she couldn't avoid it forever.

The oven timer set, Holly was about to head upstairs to make sure Mum was okay when the back door opened and Clayton came in, bringing a rush of cold air with him.

'You've got green bits stuck in your jumper,' Holly said, smiling. Clayton was the kind of man who made you smile. He certainly made Mum smile.

'Hedge trimmings. Spring has sprung, Holly. The earth's moving and I'm moving with it, here, there, and everywhere. A few more weeks and they'll be wanting their lawns done. As will your mother.'

Clayton flashed his brown eyes at Holly in a comical way. She laughed. After Dad died, they'd needed help to keep Spindlewood's huge wrap-around garden under control, and its undulating lawns that rose steeply uphill at the back of the house had caused every gardener they'd had to take a sharp intake of breath, Clayton included. Which was how he and Mum had met, of course.

'Mum's upstairs somewhere,' Holly said.

'She texted to say she was in. Can I go up?'

'Clayton, you don't have to ask.' Holly raised her eyes.

Why he hadn't moved in ages ago she had no idea. Mum was 'taking things slowly', Holly understood that, but there was slow and there was standing still for so long she was in danger of going backwards. Mum hadn't said whether they'd discussed living together, but surely the subject must have come up. It was obvious that Clayton would move in with Mum rather than the other way round. His own house, Mistletoe Cottage, in the heart of the village, was really cute and pretty but also tiny, whereas

Spindlewood had bags of space to spare. It never felt empty, though. It never had, even when it was just Mum and Holly. And when she'd been away at university, Holly had the impression that her mother never found the house too big or too lonely.

But — and here was a very big but — there might be physically enough room for all of them here, but if — no, *when* — Clayton moved in, it would, Holly imagined, be like a sort of honeymoon at first. And nothing was guaranteed to spoil it more than a daughter underfoot, never mind a . . . well, never mind.

Holly loved coming home to Spindlewood. It would always *be* home, no matter where else she happened to be laying her head at the time. But when you went off to university, it was kind of understood that you didn't move back in with your parents afterwards. It wasn't supposed to work like that, not unless there were unusual circumstances.

Okay, her own circumstances were slightly unusual, but that shouldn't stop her continuing her independence and getting a place of her own. But where, was the question. And how could she afford it on her wages from The Ginger Cat? It would require some serious thought, that was obvious.

Mum and Clayton were on their way downstairs, Mum laughing at something Clayton said. Perhaps they might have wanted to stay up there, but with her in the house . . . She shook her head to remove the mind-picture, fast. It underlined the truth, though, that she should ship out as soon as possible and leave Mum and Clayton to enjoy their romance in peace.

★   ★   ★

Wednesday night at The Goose and Feather was ladies' darts night, which meant the back room was full of darts players rather than the crowd Holly usually hung out with when she was

41

home. Strangely, she felt slightly disappointed, having geared herself up to walk into a bar full of people she knew and get it over with in one hit. There were a few familiar faces among the customers seated in the main bar area. One was George, a friend of a guy called Saul. Saul used to work for Clayton; Holly had had a bit of a thing with him the year before last. She'd heard he was away at agricultural college in Suffolk, having decided at the last minute against attending the one in Sussex, and Holly couldn't help being glad about that. George was with two other guys Holly vaguely recognised, and a girl called Ellen, who called out to Holly as soon as she and Carys walked in.

She had to go over and speak to them. It would be rude not to. Out came the story about taking a break from uni, as easy as wink. It left a nasty taste, but at least she was being consistent. After a bit of chat, she made her excuses as fast as she could, and joined Carys at table with a bench in the farthest corner.

'Friends of yours?' Carys said, nodding across.

'I used to hang out with them a bit.'

'I've not seen a single person I know since I came back, except you, of course.'

Holly felt mean then, not introducing Carys, but it would only have caused complications. Another time, perhaps.

Holly went to the bar and bought Carys the half of lager she'd asked for and a lime and soda for herself.

'Not drinking, then?'

'Didn't fancy it.'

'Okay.' Carys stretched out the word and accompanied it with a long, curious look at her.

Holly sighed. 'I'm pregnant.'

'Ah. You're having it?'

'Looks like it.'

'Oh wow! That's cool!'

'Keep your voice down,' Holly hissed, nudging Carys. 'And no, it is *not* cool. Cool is one thing it definitely is not. It's a bloody disaster, but I couldn't contemplate the alternative. It was never an option, not for me. Listen, Carys, you are not to tell anybody. Not a single living soul. Promise?'

'Okay, I promise,' Carys said, not entirely convincingly. 'Do Lloyd and Jo know?'

'No, and they're not to. Please, Carys?'

'Don't be a bat. If I say I won't say a word, then I won't. How far gone are you? They're going to spot it sooner or later, as will everybody else. Does your mum know?'

'Three months and counting. Yes, Mum knows, plus her boyfriend and her best friend, and now you. That's it, apart from a couple of uni friends in Birmingham. This isn't exactly a cause for celebration, you know. I don't want to be the talk of the village until I have to.'

Carys put down her glass and gave Holly a hug. 'But a baby, Holly! Aren't you just a bit excited as well as shit-scared? I know I would be. Excited as well as shit-scared, I mean.'

'You don't know how you'd be unless it happened to you.' Holly hadn't meant to sound harsh, but it was a fact. This wasn't something you could figure out in advance. 'Sorry, but you don't.'

Carys let a beat of silence fall. It didn't feel entirely comfortable to Holly, but she had thrown Carys a bit of a curveball. And then came the inevitable question, which, being Carys, came out as straight as an arrow. 'Whose is it?'

'Somebody I was with for a while, that's all.'

'Oh, I'd say you were definitely with him.' Carys widened her eyes.

Holly kept quiet. Carys might be direct, but she was sensitive enough to know when not to persist, and Holly felt grateful for that.

'I don't want being pregnant to define me,' she said.

'No, I get that. Talk about something else, shall we?'

'Actually,' Holly said, 'I could do with your advice.'

'Not about . . . ?'

'No.'

Carys downed the rest of her lager. 'My round. I'll just get them in, then you can fire away.'

★ ★ ★

The following day, Friday, Holly sat on the stone bench beside the towering stone war memorial engraved with the names of Charnley Acre's war heroes. She wasn't working today. Carys was, but she was due her lunch break in five minutes. While she waited, Holly thought about how she was going to break her latest news to Mum. It was probably best to wait until it was all finalised.

Bang on time, Carys came out of The Ginger Cat, waving at Holly as she walked towards her. She was eating a Cornish pasty, the grease-stained paper bag peeled halfway down.

'Have a bite, go on.'

Carys held the pasty out to Holly. It smelled wonderful, but she managed to resist. 'No, you're all right. It's your lunch. I've had mine.'

Five minutes later, having turned off the high street into the web of narrower streets behind, Carys stopped at one of the turn-offs.

'Parsley Street. This is the one.'

'I know it,' Holly said.

Charnley Acre wasn't a huge village. There wasn't a corner of it she wasn't familiar with. Parsley Street began with a terrace of flint cottages on either side, then the houses thinned out as the street wandered on, the spaces between them widening.

'Ta-da!' Carys stuffed the empty pasty bag into the pocket of her denim jacket and flung her arms wide.

'This one? You are kidding, right?'

'Nope. I haven't got time for mucking about. I'm due back at work in twenty.'

The house they stood in front of had

47

a slate roof with a chimney at either end and a dormer window in the centre. Below that were two more windows set in grimy-looking once-white walls. Apart from the pointed top of a peeling green-painted porch roof, there was little more to be seen, the lower part of the house being almost obscured by rampant greenery. Holly could make out sections of the brick path leading from the gate to where presumably the front door was.

'I remember this house,' she said. 'It used to look so neat, with a garden full of flowers. It's in a bit of a state, isn't it? Carys, seriously, you aren't expecting us to move in here, are you?'

'It's a touch neglected, grant you, but there's nothing we can't fix up between us. Well, me mostly, seeing as you're . . . never mind. It's part of the deal, I told you. Give it the *Homes and Gardens* treatment and we get to live here for a rent well below the going rate.'

'But not just us,' Holly said, recapping on what Carys had said in the pub last night. 'The owner's moving in, too.'

'Yep, but there's enough space so that we're not on top of each other. It'll be a laugh, three of us sharing, and Nan said Isaac's fully house-trained.' She giggled. 'She didn't exactly put it like that. She said he was a well brought-up young man, which amounts to the same thing.'

'Hang on a minute.' Holly looked at Carys. 'Are you saying you don't know this Isaac bloke personally?'

'Nope. Apparently, I met him once when we were kids but I don't remember. His mother is Nan's second cousin, or something like that, so he and I are distantly related.'

'Oh well, that makes all the difference.'

Carys gave Holly a sideways look. 'We don't have to do this . . . or *you* don't. Me, I'll take my chances. I need my independence, even if I'll only have moved half a mile from Nan and Grandad. Anyway, it could be fun, knocking this place into shape. Oh look . . . ' Carys had parted an overhanging shrub to reveal a circular china plaque attached to the front wall. '*Ashdown.* The house has got a name. Isn't that sweet?'

'Terrific. Carys, can I have some time to think about it?'

'Yep, course you can. Only don't take too long, because Nan has to let Isaac know if he's got his tenants sorted before he moves back to Charnley Acre.'

Holly walked back to The Ginger Cat with Carys, then set off along the high street in the opposite direction from home. She needed thinking time, and for some reason, although Mum would be at work and the house was empty, her head felt clearer when she was away from it.

It was strange, but when she first took the test and the result was positive, the choices before her were enormously important, obviously, but they were few and clear-cut. Now, it seemed, one decision led to another, and another, until her head hurt from trying to work it all out. But she could do this. If she stayed calm and focused, all would be well, in the end.

Last night in The Goose, she'd spoken to Carys about Mum and Clayton needing their privacy, her worries about losing her independence if she lived at home for too long, and how it would be best for all three of them if she moved out. Carys had been so excited at being able to offer a solution that Holly had been swept along with her. It seemed almost too good to be true that this distant relative of Carys's had bought the house in Parsley Street years ago and was looking for someone to share it with. Isaac had only lived there a short time, Holly heard, before he'd gone to work as an administrator in a London hospital. Disillusioned with city life, he'd secured the post of practice manager at a large medical practice in Cliffhaven. As Cliffhaven was only ten miles from Charnley Acre, it made sense for him to move back into the house.

'But isn't Isaac expecting it to be just you?' Holly had asked.

'Oh, don't worry about that. He'll be as sweet as a nut. I'll square it with Nan. She can pass on the news via Isaac's mother and he'll be over the moon about getting two lodgers for the price of one. Take it from me.' She'd thrown her head back and laughed as if she'd made a great joke, drawing smiles from around the bar.

'You make it up as you go along,' Holly had said, laughing too.

She'd noticed Carys had said two lodgers, not three. Either she'd temporarily forgotten about Holly's situation or was being diplomatic. But Carys's enthusiasm, along with her laugh, was infectious, and Holly had hardly been able to wait until today to set eyes on her future home. The state of the place had come as a shock — to her; Carys was unshockable — but as her friend had assured her on the walk back to The Ginger Cat, the work that needed doing was only cosmetic. Carys was guessing, of course. She hadn't seen inside the house either. Holly would hold her opinion until the proper viewing. She and Carys were both working tomorrow, Saturday; but on Sunday a second trip to Parsley Street was planned, by which time Carys would have acquired the keys to Ashdown. It was exciting, though. She was with Carys on that.

So, *Mum*, Holly thought, as she passed the public library and took a turning at random that led away from the high street. It only took her a minute to decide not to say anything about moving out until she'd had a look at the house. It might be a damp, crumbling tip, in which case she wouldn't want to live there; her health was mega-important now. Besides, presenting Laura with a *fait accompli* would be a whole lot easier, and kinder, than sharing a half-baked idea.

The cottages along the lane she'd

chosen were impossibly picture-book pretty, with half-timbered frontages and leaded-light windows hardly bigger than cornflake packets. It wasn't surprising the village attracted streams of summer tourists on a quest for 'bygone Sussex', as it said in the brochures. But even the increased footfall only caused a ripple in the quietness of the place, like a hand passing through a wheat field. Home or not, was this silent backwater where she really wanted to stay, for as long as it took to see this situation through?

On the other hand, she had to be practical. This wasn't the right time to be thinking about shipping out again. Independence was one thing, stupidity quite another. Besides, she really liked Carys and her take-it-or-leave-it attitude to life. They would have a lot of fun living at Ashdown. She could only hope that Isaac was a relaxed sort of bloke and wouldn't fuss about the girls hogging the bathroom or leaving knickers drying on the radiators — if there were any radiators.

Her mind refused to form an image of what Isaac might look like. All she knew — all Carys knew — was that he was around thirty, and that was it. He could be five foot three with a prematurely receding hairline, or a big hairy bear of a man, or any combination of the two. He might be morosely unsociable, or he might fall into the house hammered most nights of the week and tow his drunken mates home to crash out on the sofa.

She was letting her imagination run riot now. Isaac's choice of career in the health service indicated that he was at least a halfway decent, regular guy, and he had given her somewhere to live, even if he didn't yet know it. She would stop trying to second-guess him. If Carys had her way and they moved into the house in around two weeks' time, they would still have another month before they met Isaac. He wasn't taking up his new post until the first week of May and was staying in

London till then.

Holly's finances were high on the list of things she should be thinking about. She'd pushed all that to the back of her mind, believing she had plenty of time; but if she was going to house-share, she had to face reality. There'd be bills to pay and general living expenses, on top of the generously small amount of rent Carys said they'd be paying. She and Mum had sat down at the computer and tracked down information about the allowances she might be entitled to claim from the state, and she'd picked up the relevant leaflets from the health centre. But all that depended on certain factors she hadn't yet dared give voice to.

Mum had also said she needn't pay anything towards her keep and that she'd help with Holly's other expenses, but that was when she'd been expecting her to live at home. Besides, Spindle-wood might be a beautiful house and they were lucky to have it, but it was expensive to run, even with Clayton doing the constant repairs it needed. She couldn't expect Mum to support her, not on her teacher's salary. It wouldn't be fair, and Holly didn't want to do that.

But she had her wages from The Ginger Cat, plus tips. Not a fortune, but enough — hopefully — to get by on. She was young and strong; there was no reason why she shouldn't carry on working almost up to the end, providing Jo and Lloyd didn't kick her out first.

Holly walked on to the end of the row of cottages. There was a tiny sweet shop on the corner, its window filled with dusty jars of humbugs, sherbet pips, and Pontefract cakes, giving it an old-fashioned vibe that charmed the village children and pleased the visitors.

Ducking beneath the low lintel of the doorway, she went in and bought a bar of chocolate. It was dark inside the shop. At least the elderly man behind the counter didn't immediately recognise her and wonder out loud why she was back in Charnley Acre, although she'd been coming in here practically all her life.

Hurrying out again before the penny dropped, Holly retraced her steps back towards the high street, nibbling the chocolate as she went.

★   ★   ★

'Oh, look at the fireplace! Have you ever seen one like that?'

Holly laughed. The fireplace Carys was exclaiming over had shiny brown and beige mottled tiles surrounding a fitted gas fire so old it must surely have been condemned by the gas people long ago.

'Yes, all right.' Carys was laughing too now. 'It's pig-awful, but it does lend a certain retro character, don't you think?'

'No, I don't think. The rest isn't bad, though.'

Holly looked around the living room.

It was long and narrow, stretching from back to front of the house. Behind the sofa there was, thankfully, a radiator covered in chipped cream gloss paint. The furniture looked a bit shabby, but at least there was furniture, and the flat black face of a large-screen TV stared out incongruously from a scratched pine table in the corner.

'Satellite?' she said, turning to Carys.

'Yep. Dish is round the back.'

'Wi-fi?'

'You don't want much, do you?' Carys raised her eyes. 'Not yet, but Isaac said it's the first thing he's doing once he gets back, as well as having the outside of the house fixed up.'

'And this is according to Isaac himself?'

''Course. Via his mum, via Nan, via . . . '

'Via the man who sweeps the streets.'

'What's this bumpy stuff?' Carys was rubbing a hand over the grubby magnolia-emulsioned wall.

'Woodchip wallpaper. Spindlewood

was full of it until Mum and Dad scraped it off.'

'We could do that, then.'

'No,' Holly said. 'Start taking that off and half the wall will come with it, then it'll have to be re-plastered. We'll paint over it, if we're allowed.'

'I told you. Isaac's happy for us to brighten the place up any way we want.'

'I bet he is.' Holly pulled a face. 'It'll save him a job.' She realised how mean she sounded. 'I am grateful to him, though. You will tell him that, won't you? Through your nan, I mean.'

'If you like. Good, though, isn't it, the house?'

Holly nodded. She was surer than ever now that she wanted to live here, with Carys and their mystery landlord. They'd looked all around. On the other side of the central hallway was a room that was the twin of this one. A long refectory-style table occupied most of it, with an assortment of chairs around it. They'd already decided they wouldn't need a dining room, but having two reception rooms would be useful, and would mean that when all three of them were in, they wouldn't get under each other's feet.

The kitchen was spacious and bright, and had a new-looking cooker and fridge. The fitted pine cupboards were dated but functional. There was an old-fashioned larder with some ancient jars of home-made jam and a few tins on the otherwise empty shelves, and tacked on at the back was a small utility room with a stone floor, a washing machine, a chest freezer, and a sink. The kitchen door opened onto the back garden.

Upstairs were three bedrooms, all of decent sizes. The biggest one over-looked the front of the house and had a range of fitted wardrobes: Isaac's room, left just as it was since he was last here. The double bed was made up with a blue and white striped duvet, a stack of paperbacks teetered on top of an old dining chair doing duty as a bedside table, and there were pens, notepads, a couple of sober-looking ties, and a handful of loose change strewn around the base of an old-fashioned mirror on top of a chest of drawers.

Holly and Carys had agreed on the two back bedrooms, currently with single beds which they'd replace with doubles. Next to Isaac's room was the bathroom. It was clean and functional, with a shower over the bath. The fittings were blush pink, but as Carys said, you couldn't have everything.

'I wonder what's the attic's like.' Holly had gazed up a steep, narrow staircase.

'Spidery, probably.' Carys had pulled a face. 'Let's not look now. It might come in handy, though, the extra room.' She'd widened her eyes and looked pointedly at Holly.

Holly had dipped her gaze. *Not that conversation, not yet. Maybe not ever.*

Carys had looked serious, unusually so for her. 'It is happening, Holly.'

'I know it is, and I'm dealing with it.'

Carys had nodded but said no more.

4

Holly had planned to break the news to her mother about moving out as soon as she got home, but Laura had left a note on the kitchen table to say she'd gone out with Clayton and not to wait on lunch. She didn't come home until gone six, wearing a smile as wide as the ocean and looking all sparkly, as she always did when she'd spent time with Clayton.

And then, just as Holly had psyched herself up for a meaningful chat, Mum said she had lessons to prep for Monday. 'You don't mind, do you? How was your walk with Carys?'

'Good, thanks.'

'I like Carys. She's lovely.'

This would have been a good introduction to a potentially thorny conversation, had Mum not taken herself off to the dining room. By the time she'd finished her work, Holly was too tired to do anything but chill out with her in front of the telly, whilst smiling over constant texts from Carys about her ideas for decorating Ashdown which became increasingly ambitious as the evening went on.

Now it was Monday morning, and business at The Ginger Cat was steady, if not that busy. Most of the customers were middle-aged women, catching up with friends over coffee and cake. Holly was working but Carys had the day off. As she'd put on her cat-printed tabard over her jeans and blue cotton shirt, she'd carried out her habitual check in the long mirror in the area off the kitchen, noting with satisfaction that she looked more or less the same as usual. The middle buttons on her shirt pulled on the buttonholes a bit, and her face seemed fuller and a bit flushed, but the differences were negligible. The jeans still fitted, just. She had some at home in a larger size that she could swap them for later. Some of the aromas from the cooking of the light lunches, especially the poached eggs and the spinach and mushroom omelettes, could induce a swell of nausea, but it soon passed. All in all, she was doing pretty well, considering.

It was while there was a lull in service and she was chatting to Jo behind the counter that she heard the faint tune playing from her phone.

'Go. Answer it,' Jo said. 'We're not exactly run off our feet.'

'Thanks.'

Holly went through to the back and took her phone from the pocket of her cardigan. 'Bethany! Hiya!'

This was a surprise, a good one. She'd kept in contact with Bethany and her other close friends at uni, but mostly it was by text or email, and she hadn't liked to impose too much by phoning. Life in Birmingham already seemed to belong to the past, though she wished it didn't.

'How are you? Are you showing yet?'

Holly giggled. 'Sshh! No, thank God.' She slipped out of the open kitchen door and stood against the wall, facing the yard with its neat stacks of crates and the small garden beyond. The brickwork felt pleasantly warm on her back. 'How are you, Beth? How's everyone? What gossip have I missed?'

Holly's mood dipped as she heard about the new girl, a pharmacy student, who had moved into her old room in the shared house. Apparently she was 'a real laugh'. Oh, and Amber had got off with a geography student during a raucous night out and ended up at his place with no memory as to how she'd got there, or what happened in between. Bethany's hilarity over this incident seemed to Holly way out of line. Before, she'd have joined in the hilarity, no problem. Before . . .

Holly sighed. Beth heard. 'Are you really okay, Holly? Do you want me to come down and visit in the Easter hols? Oh no, hang about. Mum wants me to go to Cornwall with her and my sister. I could get out of it, though.'

'Don't you dare. Cornwall will be amazing, and I'm fine, honestly. Anyway, I'll be up to my armpits in paint and varnish if Carys has her way.' She'd given Bethany a quick rundown of her house-sharing plans. 'See you in the summer, though?'

'Yep, deffo.' A hesitation, then, 'Holly?'

'What?'

'Have you heard from Lorcan? Has he texted or anything?'

'No. Not a whisper.' And how grateful she was for that.

'Look, I wasn't going to say anything, but . . .'

A small silence.

'*What*, Beth?'

'Lorcan came and found me. He was waiting outside the lecture theatre. He asked where you were.'

'Oh God, what did you say?'

'Don't worry, I said I had no idea. He didn't believe me, of course, and as I walked away I heard him ask another student — not one of our lot — if you'd left uni, and she said you hadn't been in lectures for ages and she was pretty sure you'd gone. What I don't get is, if he's that interested, why he doesn't just ring you?'

'Probably because he knows what sort of reception he'd get.'

Another pause then, while Bethany waited for more. When it wasn't forthcoming, she said, 'Holly, I know you never said Lorcan was the father, but it's fairly obvious. You may have dumped him months before — or he dumped you, whatever — but if you ask me, it was always a case of unfinished business between the two of you.'

Holly's throat suddenly felt acid with bile, and it was nothing to do with the smell of cooking. But Bethany was on her side. She wasn't being nosey or trying to stir things by mentioning Lorcan; she was just warning her. It wasn't Beth's fault that Holly hadn't shared the intimate details of her relationship with Lorcan. With so little to go on, Beth was understandably making it up as she went along.

Least said, soonest mended. To think she'd always believed that. Holly gave a little humourless laugh.

'What's funny?' said Bethany.

'Nothing. Nothing at all. Look, I've got to go. If he comes poking around again, you won't say where I am, will you? Or anything about . . . ?'

'No way, and nor will any of the others. We've got your back, no worries.'

'I know. Thanks, Beth. Talk to you soon. Give my love to everyone.'

Holly felt bereft when the call ended. She continued to stand by the wall for a few minutes, wondering if she was already out of Bethany's mind as she rushed off to another lecture, or to meet friends in the refectory. Holly had been happy in Birmingham. She'd been apprehensive as well as excited, leaving home to begin her first year, but it had turned out even better than she'd hoped — her English course, sharing a house with new people in a strange city, the whole student life thing. She'd even enjoyed working four evenings a week on a supermarket checkout, because she knew she wouldn't be doing it forever, and the money came in handy.

Would she really be returning to pick up where she'd left off, or was that it, dream over? It was obvious that everyone else was thinking it was, even if they never actually said so.

As for Lorcan, Holly refused to worry about him. Beth was right; if he was really intent on tracking her down, he'd have phoned or texted long before this. He wouldn't have gone sneaking about. That was probably just idle curiosity on his part. There was still the odd moment — in the middle of the night, mostly — when the old longing came back. But it wasn't real. Muscle memory, that was all. After what happened back in January, she couldn't have made it any plainer that Lorcan was to stay away from her.

She heard the café door open and

close a few times. The lunchtime rush had begun. Lloyd was in the kitchen when Holly went back in, slicing cucumber and tomatoes for the salads and sandwiches.

'Okay?' he said, regarding Holly with some degree of curiosity.

'Yep.' Holly put her phone back in the pocket of her cardigan which was hanging over the back of a chair.

'You're looking a bit peaky, I thought.'

'*Peaky?*'

'Pale, then. Bit washed-out.'

'Oh, nice.' Holly raised her eyes and grinned. Flushed one minute, pale the next. She made a mental note to slap on a bit of make-up tomorrow to disguise whatever else her face might betray. 'I'm fine. Just need an early night, that's all.'

★ ★ ★

'Mum, how would you feel about me moving out?'

Laura let the door of the dishwasher swing shut with a clunk. 'One day you'll want a place of your own, a home for you and your child, of course you will. But that's way down the line. Let's not think about it yet.'

Child. The word was enough to send needles of anxiety all the way up the backs of her legs. As she'd suspected, her mother had a certain scenario in her mind which wouldn't be easy to dispel. Holly rested both hands on the back of a chair and pressed on.

'No, I don't mean in the future. I mean now. I know I've only just come home, but look at me. I'm fit and healthy, so there's no reason why I should still be getting under your feet here.'

Before Laura could protest, Holly launched into the story about Carys wanting to move out of her nan's, and how she really wanted Holly to share with her, and about the house called Ashdown which was just perfect because it was in Charnley Acre, which meant she'd hardly be moving at all, geographically speaking. She found herself overemphasising Isaac's need to fill his empty rooms with lodgers, but needs must, if her mother was to be convinced.

Mum's hand strayed to her mouth and stayed there for a long, thoughtful moment. Her blue-grey eyes — the same as Holly's — showed a mixture of emotions: shock, doubt, and, Holly was upset to realise, hurt.

'Mum?' Holly went to Laura and put her arms round her. 'It'll be okay.'

She wasn't sure what she meant by that, because there wasn't much about this situation that was ever going to be okay. Hugging her back, Mum smiled, although Holly sensed it cost her something to do it.

'Holly, what Carys wants, and this distant cousin of hers with a house to fill, doesn't come into it. My only concern is you. They'll find someone else to share if needs be.'

'I know, but I want to do it. I've

thought about it loads and it's the right thing. Sorry Mum, it isn't that I don't want to live with you, it's more that you need your own life, you and Clayton. And I have been away to university, so it's not as if I don't know how to look after myself, is it?'

'That's debatable.' Mum widened her eyes.

Holly looked at the floor, but when she looked up, Mum was smiling properly. 'Sorry, that was below the belt, so to speak.' They both giggled.

It was going to be all right. She just had to stay focussed.

'Yeah, well, these things happen.' Another meaningless remark.

'Indeed they do, my love.' Laura pressed the button on the dishwasher. 'Right then. Let's go in there and talk about this properly, shall we?'

Holly followed her mother to the living room.

'This is my fault,' Mum said, sitting down on the squishy plum-coloured sofa.

Holly, next to her mother, pulled a cushion onto her lap and hugged it to her. 'How d'you mean?'

'For not saying what I was thinking. I had it all worked out in my head. You were coming home — well, you did that — and I was going to look after you, and the baby when it came, and we'd do up the spare bedroom next to yours as a nursery. I thought maybe later we could even do something with the attic and turn it into a playroom or an extra bathroom.' She stopped and looked at Holly. 'But as I said, that was all in my mind and we hadn't actually talked about any of that. Clearly, we were on different pages, and I'm sorry.'

'No, Mum. Don't say sorry.' Holly sat up straight and clutched the cushion tighter. 'It was me. I wasn't on any page. All I wanted to do was get home. I hadn't thought any further than that, not then.'

This wasn't quite true, but she didn't want to upset her mother further by telling her she'd been planning to move out all along, except at the time she had nowhere to go.

Mum nodded thoughtfully. Holly hoped desperately that she wasn't going to move onto the subject of the baby's father again. She didn't. All she said was that perhaps Holly could treat moving into Ashdown as a trial, and if it didn't work out, she could come back to Spindlewood. Holly agreed. It felt safe to consider it like that — not that she needed 'safe', but you never knew. You never knew much at all, really, even when you thought you did.

'Anyway, what did you mean about me and Clayton?' Mum said. 'What's he got to do with the price of fish?'

Holly laughed. 'Oh Mum, you're hopeless! Anyone can see you two ought to be together full-time. Why don't you ask him to move in and be done with it? He must be desperate for you to say something.'

Mum tapped the side of her nose. 'And who's to say I haven't said anything? If you must know, we talked about it and we both decided we were happy as we are. If it ain't broke, don't fix it.'

Holly was about to make a joke about all the repairs Clayton had done on Spindlewood, but her mother's expression was serious now.

'This is not about me, or Clayton. It's about you. You can't do this without support, Holly. I know you think you can, but it's hard, especially for a single girl, and it will get harder as the months go by. I do wish you'd stay here. I want to be around for the birth, if you'll let me, and afterwards, when it gets even harder. Living in a house-share like a student is not the ideal environment for a pregnant woman, never mind one who's just given birth. And how is this Isaac going to take to having a baby screaming in the middle of the night to be fed? Does he know, by the way?'

'No, not yet.'

Mum said nothing but the look on her face said it all. Holly's spirits plunged. She'd thought Mum was coming round to the idea of her moving into Ashdown.

'Well, there it is.' Laura folded her arms and sat back. 'You're an adult. You don't need my permission to do whatever you want to do.' Hard words, but the overbrightness of her eyes told a different story.

'I thought we'd just agreed I'd give it a try?' Holly said. 'Now it sounds like you're going back on that.' She heard the juvenile sulkiness in her voice but felt powerless to stop it.

'I wish you'd reconsider, that's all.' Laura wasn't looking at Holly. Her gaze was fixed on the landscape painting above the fireplace.

There seemed nothing left to say. It was so dispiriting having Mum so against the idea, when she'd been so looking forward to moving into Ashdown with Carys and Isaac. Actually, she was still looking forward to it. Her mother's disapproval had put a dampener on it, but she'd come round. She understood, deep down, why Holly was so set on doing this.

After a minute, Holly got up from the sofa. 'I'm going up for a bath.' Then, when there was no reply, 'You okay, Mum?'

'Mm?' Laura seemed distracted, and a little upset, which made Holly feel guilty. But then she smiled. 'Of course. Enjoy your bath. Put some of my Jo Malone in. It smells gorgeous.'

Holly had put her pyjamas on and was towel-drying the ends of her hair when Mum tapped on her bedroom door and put her head round.

'Are you coming back down? I'm making hot chocolate.'

'Ooh yes, make me one. Please.'

Laura ducked back, then seemingly changed her mind and came right into the room. 'I shall want to come and see this house. Before you move in, that is.'

'Of course. Whenever you like.' It was progress, a whole heap of progress, but Holly wasn't so naïve that she thought Mum was entirely happy about her plans.

'Holly . . .'

'I know, I know.' Holly held up her hands. 'Sorry, Mum. I've already brought you enough worry, but I won't be far away, will I? We'll probably see as much of each other as we do now.' Laura pulled a face. 'Okay, maybe not quite as much, but thanks, Mum, for being so cool about it.'

'Well, I wouldn't quite go that far.' She hesitated. 'This is difficult for me, too. The whole thing. You've no idea.'

When Mum had gone back downstairs, Holly sat and thought, for the millionth time, how something so seemingly straightforward could suddenly become so complicated.

* * *

Easter week arrived, bringing with it streamers of cloud tugged across sharp blue skies by a sly wind that stung Holly's eyes as she walked down to The Ginger Cat on the mornings she was working. Lloyd kept a constant check on the weather, examining the sky to see if there was any chance of an April shower to bring the customers hurrying in. Not that they needed any encouragement; The Ginger Cat's hot cross buns, part-baked on the premises, were always a draw, and Holly served little else with the teas and coffees, especially mid-morning.

Laura's school was closed for the holidays, and on Good Friday Holly gave her mother a guided tour of Ashdown.

'It's not very big, is it?' Mum said as they reached the bedroom that was to be Holly's.

'It's fine. It'll take a double bed, when I get one in here,' Holly said, pretending not to understand the implication behind Mum's remark.

'I suppose the cot can go down this side, under the window, but not if there's any possibility of a draught. You'll have to make sure of that.'

'I know.' Holly walked out of the room, taking a deep breath as she stood on the landing while, deep down in the secret part of her mind, her emotions rolled and flipped like waves in a storm.

'We'll go shopping next week then, shall we?' Mum came up behind her. Then, seeing Holly's face, she added, 'For a new bed, I mean, that's all. Your other bed should stay at home, I think, don't you?'

'Yes, okay. You can help me choose, but I don't expect you to fork out for a bed, Mum, honestly.'

'I can't see how you're going to afford one otherwise. It'll be my housewarming present to you.'

'I've got the money Dad left me for university, and my wages from The Ginger Cat,' Holly said.

'Yes, and you'll need every penny.'

This was true. Tins of paint and stuff were one thing; a major purchase like a bed was quite another. If this was going to work, she'd have to stay grounded.

'Thanks, Mum.' Holly followed Laura back downstairs. 'I mean it.

Thanks for, well, you know . . . ' Tears filled her eyes.

'Oh, Holly, don't.' Mum hugged her. 'You'll start me off in a minute, and believe me, I don't take a lot of starting these days.'

Really? Holly was smitten by guilt. She hadn't seen Mum cry, not over her and the situation, but knowing she was doing that in private made it worse somehow.

Yet this was supposed to be a happy day. The sun was shining in through the windows of Ashdown, mauve and yellow crocuses had managed to push their way through the muddle of vegetation in the garden, and the weekend after next, the time she'd agreed with Carys, she'd actually be living here. She couldn't wait.

'It's a good house, though, isn't it?'

'It's a very good house, and I'm sure you'll be happy here. You and Carys, plus whoever else comes along later.' She hesitated. 'Holly, are you sure you don't want to know whether it's a girl or a boy? They will tell you at the next scan, if you want them to.'

'I don't want them to. I don't have to ask, do I?'

'No, of course you don't. If it was me, I wouldn't want to know either. It spoils the surprise.'

Stop, please!

Holly opened the front door. It creaked where it was stiff from underuse. 'Shall we go home now? I promised to Facetime Beth while she's in Cornwall, and tonight I'm meeting Carys at the pub. We're going to draw up a plan of action and make a list of all the stuff we want to do before we move in.'

'Yes, let's go. Emily's coming round later.'

'Not Clayton?'

'We aren't joined at the hip, you know.'

★   ★   ★

'Ooh, I *love* that!'

Holly was gazing at the turquoise

84

wall in the living room of Ashdown, the wall with the dubious fireplace in the middle of it.

'Do you? Thank Gawd for that.' Carys blew upwards, ruffling the bit of hair that had escaped from her makeshift turban made out of a tea-towel with a faded map of Sussex on it. 'It's come out tons brighter than the square on the tin, but it'll darken down in time.'

'No, I think it's great. Goes so well with the rest. And it leads the eye away from the fireplace.'

The other three walls had been painted silvery grey, the door and the deep wooden skirting brilliant white. Holly and Carys had spent four days — between shifts at The Ginger Cat — painting this room. It had taken ages and used up so much paint because of the lumps and bumps in the woodchip wallpaper and general dents in the plaster underneath it, but the result had been worth it.

'We'll have to get new curtains,'

Carys said, wrinkling her nose.

The curtains at the windows either end of the room were covered in orange and russet-coloured flowers which could be chrysanthemums; it was hard to tell. Isaac couldn't care much about his home surroundings, otherwise he'd have already replaced them.

'They can wait. We can't do it all at once,' Holly said, thinking of the expense.

'Why spoil the ship for tuppence-worth of tar? as my Grandad says. I'll look for some cheap material online. Nan will run them up for us, no problem.'

'Your nan's a saint,' Holly said, sitting down. Her legs ached from standing at work all day.

'You won't say that when you see what's on the upstairs landing.'

'Why? What is it?'

'Go up and see.' Carys pulled the tea-towel off her head. Her dark, glossy bob immediately fell into perfect shape.

Holly's hair felt greasy and lank in

comparison. Pregnancy was meant to improve your hair, wasn't it? Another old wives' tale. She went upstairs and saw what Carys meant. The new addition to the landing was a dark wood three-drawer chest, inlaid with Oriental figures in a bridge-heavy landscape. The drawers had horrible brassy handles. It might have been fashionable once, but now it looked distinctly depressing.

Carys came upstairs. 'Horrendous, isn't it? Nan says we can keep all the extra sheets and stuff in it. She got Grandad to bring it round earlier.' She looked at Holly. 'Well, you can't say no, can you? To be honest, I think she's been angling to get rid of the thing for years.'

'Couldn't she have hung on till Bonfire Night?'

Carys laughed and slapped Holly on the arm. 'Yeah, nice one. Mind you, you could give it a coat of paint and keep the baby's stuff in it. It's got to go somewhere.'

Holly shrugged and escaped to her bedroom. She heard Carys say something about starting dinner. It was obvious that Carys was as confused as Mum over Holly's refusal to talk about the baby, but it was the only way she could cope with all that was going on in her mind, and her heart.

Once in her bedroom, Holly relaxed. The late afternoon sun streamed in between the lilac and white curtains. She drew them back fully, letting the soft spring light flood the room. All was new and bright in here. The walls were painted in the same grey as downstairs — Carys's room had it too; there'd been a special offer on — and Mum had insisted on buying the curtains as well as the lovely, comfy new bed. She'd wanted to buy new sets of bedding, too, but Holly hadn't let her. Instead, she'd brought one set from her old bed, and another they'd found at the bottom of the pile in the airing cupboard at home.

Pulling her navy-blue jumper over her head and throwing it on the chair,

Holly performed her daily ritual of self-examination in the front of the long mirror on the wardrobe door. It was getting too warm for the jumper now, but since it was her longest, baggiest item of clothing, she'd have to put up with it for a few more weeks. Worn over the larger size jeans or a succession of stretchy jeggings in varying shades of black and grey, it covered a multitude of sins. Sins that belonged only in a small part to her, the rest lodging firmly elsewhere.

Best not to think about that.

She stood sideways on, turning her head to look in the mirror. There was definitely enough of a bump now for it to deserve its name. No longer could she pass it off as over-indulgence in her favourite chocolate brownies — to herself, or to anyone else who showed an interest. Which, luckily, nobody had. Yet. She had to hang onto that job at The Ginger Cat as long as possible. Having her income drastically cut didn't bear thinking about, and she wouldn't think about it, not until she had to. Jo and Lloyd would be fine about her condition, she was sure of that. They were some of the most non-judgmental people she knew. But they might not be so keen when they found out she planned to stay on until she could no longer squeeze between the tables or behind the counter.

Holly opened the window and leaned on the sill to look out. The back garden, like the front, was showing signs of spring. Buds were breaking, spears of bulbs pierced the soil, and bright new grass had begun to spread across the bald patches of the newly emerged lawn. Clayton, bless him, had given up a half a day to come and hack down the worst of the overgrowth and clear the weeds and general accumulation of rubbish. Typically, he'd refused to accept a penny in payment, even though it was Carys who'd offered it. And he'd promised to come back to do more when he had time. Mum's friend, Emily, had a garden table and chairs in her shed, now replaced by new ones, and she'd promised those for when the weather was warm enough to sit out.

Funny, though. She should feel lucky and grateful to have all these lovely, generous people around her. And she did, of course. Yet, at the same time, there was this weird feeling that it was all happening to somebody else and she was just an onlooker. Hormones, her mother would say. Those damn things had one hell of a lot to answer for.

★　★　★

As they sat over dinner in the kitchen, Carys was unusually quiet. There were shadows under her eyes.

'Are you sleeping okay?' Holly asked, scraping the crispy bits of lasagne out of the dish.

Carys looked up from her plate, surprised. 'Yeah. Like a top. Why?'

'No reason.' Holly shrugged and smiled. 'I just thought.' Nobody wanted to be told they looked tired.

Holly thought about last night, and the faint but unmistakeable sounds of Carys moving about in the room next to hers, yet she hadn't gone to the bathroom. Last night, and the night before that, and several nights last week. But she said no more, except to instruct Carys to go and put her feet up while she washed up.

'I won't argue with that,' Carys said. 'We were towering busy today, and a load of mums came in and brought their kids with them. The table was swimming in juice by the time they went. Little brats.' She stood up from the table. 'Your phone went off just now. A message.'

'Did it?' Holly hadn't heard. She wiped her hands on her jumper and fetched her phone from the shelf in the hall, frowning at the screen.

'Anything interesting?' Carys stopped in the doorway.

'Nope.' She dropped the phone onto the table.

'Nothing interesting ever happens,'

Carys said, with a melodramatic toss of her head.

When Carys had gone, Holly took up the phone, stabbed at it to delete the message, then switched it off. But not before the words had imprinted themselves on her brain.

Am I forgiven yet? I really hope so because I love you, Holly. I miss you. Come back soon. Lorcan xxx

5

Monday morning, and Holly was feeling crabby. For a student of English, it wasn't the most elegant of words, but as a label for the way she felt, it hit the spot dead centre. Crabby. And grouchy and miserable and spotty and fat and sick. And *hot*. That coffee machine belched so much steam, and the double oven was on in the kitchen. Outside, it was like summer, and her forehead had broken out in a sweat even before she got here.

The oversized grey cotton sweatshirt she'd taken to wearing — borrowed from Mum — was lighter than the navy jumper but still too warm on a morning like this. Perhaps she should give up her privacy as a bad job and swan around the village wearing her bump like a badge of honour. Why shouldn't she? Because she didn't want to, that was why. This was her private life; she didn't need any other reason.

It hadn't helped matters to have overheard a conversation between two women while she was clearing their table. 'My Leanne takes it all in her stride, you know. Three babies now, and she's sailed through every pregnancy, just like that.' The speaker had snapped her fingers in the air.

'Perhaps she'd like to sail through mine then,' Holly had muttered under her breath.

When she'd gone for her latest routine check-up, the nurse at the clinic — a no-nonsense sixtyish woman with a determined chin who Holly bet had been hockey captain in her day — had used phrases like 'coming along nicely' and 'Mum and baby on tip-top form'. Holly begged to differ.

She shoved a chair back into place at a table recently vacated by two teenage girls who obviously didn't give a stuff, judging by the mess they'd made with two skinny cappuccinos and one shared chocolate muffin. The squeak of the chair legs made her clench her teeth and drew a curious glance from Lloyd. Well, Holly didn't give a stuff either.

In theory, the foul mood she was in made no sense at all. She'd had a brilliant weekend. She'd worked on Saturday until two, but the time had flown because Carys had been on duty as well. In the afternoon, Emily had invited her and Mum over to her house, Cloud Cottage, for a cream tea with home-made scones and jam, and proper clotted cream from the farm shop. Emily, who was Mum's age and divorced, had met a new bloke online and wanted to show him off. Not in person, disappointingly, but via his social media profile and a couple of shots Emily had managed to sneak in when they'd been to Bodiam Castle the weekend before.

Holly was constantly surprised that Emily hadn't found her soulmate before now, especially as she was a journalist on the *Cliffhaven News* and got to meet loads of different people all the time. She was confident and really pretty, and very funny when she got talking. Perhaps this new bloke would be the one. Holly hoped so, and so did Mum. All three of them had giggled like schoolgirls on Saturday; it had been such a fun afternoon.

Sunday had been spent at home with Carys, putting the finishing touches to Ashdown. They'd changed the old curtains in both downstairs rooms for new ones in a cream and blue checked fabric — run up, as promised, by Carys's nan — Carys balancing precariously on a step-ladder which looked as if the rungs might give way at any moment while Holly fed the material up to her. They'd added cheap but cheerful throws to the sofa and cushions donated by Holly's mother. Carys had even given the old wooden bathroom cabinet a coat of paint.

There was still plenty that could be done, but even Carys was bored with it now. They'd both agreed that Isaac could carry on where they'd left off, although as he hadn't bothered before, it didn't seem likely he would now. But, as Carys said, you never could tell, and they should just wait and see.

The two of them had gone to The Goose and Feather last night. Carys had been all for going somewhere further afield in her battered but endlessly useful little Fiat, until Holly had said that there was no point in both of them going alcohol-free. It was bad enough when it was just her, and so they'd stayed local.

Some of the old gang had been there: George, and other casual friends Holly used to hang out with. But now she felt out of the loop, and a tiny bit awkward with them. They were in the room at the back, playing pool. Holly had ducked in and said 'hi' and they'd greeted her as if she'd never been away, and nothing had changed. And then one of the girls, Susie, had surprised her.

'Hey, Holly, you're having a baby, right?'

Shock would have described it better than surprise. Holly had felt herself staring, open-mouthed, and then she'd nodded.

'Cool,' Susie had said, while George had given her the thumbs-up, and the others had smiled across at her before carrying on with their game, as if this was all commonplace stuff, and nothing to break sweat about.

Holly had automatically glanced down. She was wearing a dark purple tunic over grey leggings, the only normal-looking outfit she could get into now that was fit for a night out. She hadn't seemed particularly bulbous when she'd checked in the mirror earlier.

'How do they *know*?' she'd complained to Carys when they'd sat down in the bar area.

'It is a *bit* noticeable, Holl, when you stand sideways.' Carys had looked apologetic. 'It's only because you were

99

so slim to start with. It wouldn't show this early on somebody bigger. And you did suddenly pitch up in the middle of term. Doesn't take a genius.'

Once she'd got over the shock of people knowing about her condition without her having told them, strangely enough she'd felt relieved rather than annoyed.

'I wanted . . . ' She'd stopped and looked at Carys.

'. . . to be in control. Yes, I know you did. Just take it as it comes, sweetheart, that's all you can do. And be *happy*, Holly.' Carys had raised her glass of lager. 'To baby Engleby. Or whatever his name is.'

Holly had laughed so much at Carys's toast that she'd forgotten to tell her to keep her voice down. It would have been too late, anyway, judging by the smiles that came from the occupants of the nearby tables. At least she didn't know any of them.

They'd gone on laughing all evening. Carys had the knack of being able to make all your troubles disappear; the best asset a friend could have. And by the time they'd arrived back at Ashdown and Holly had fallen into bed, she'd felt bone-tired but happy, and ready to take on the world.

A world which seemed a very different place this morning. Well, she'd have to shake herself out of it, that was all.

'Could I order? I'm a bit strapped for time.'

Holly turned to see a guy at one of the small tables by the window. In fact, he wasn't properly at the table; he was still standing, shrugging off a black bomber jacket and hooking it over the back of the chair. Talk about impatient. He could see she had a tray full of dirty crockery.

'A 'please' would be nice,' she said, sensing her own bad temper notching up instead of climbing down.

'What?' He frowned, pulled out the chair and sat down. 'Oh, right. Sorry. But can you hurry, only I've got to be somewhere, and it's turned out to be farther than I thought.'

He fished a mobile phone from his pocket, glared at it and put it back again. Still no 'please'. Not even a smile. And although she hated herself for the thought, she had an idea it would be something worth waiting for.

'I'll be with you as soon as I've dealt with this. Have a look at the menu.' She nearly added 'sir' but it would have come out as sarcastically as intended, so best not. She needed this job, and Lloyd had ears like a bat.

As she went behind the counter and deposited the tray, she surreptitiously eyed the guy at the table. The removal of the jacket had revealed a black polo shirt buttoned neatly at the neck, well-shaped arms, strong shoulders, and a lean torso. He wasn't especially tall, no more than about five-nine. He had dark blond hair, short, but long enough on top to be nicely ruffled, grey eyes, and the type of face you wouldn't automatically describe as conventionally handsome — his nose was too large for that — but attractive in a brooding, quirky sort of way. Holly couldn't help laughing inwardly at herself. She still had some normal responses left then.

He ordered a bacon and sausage baguette and a pot of tea. She almost pointed out that if he was in that much of a rush, a non-cooked item might have been the better option, but decided she couldn't care less whether he was late or not. She tried not to notice his meaningful gaze in her direction as she waited for Lloyd to griddle the sausage and bacon, then made up the tray with cutlery, napkin and the pot of tea, taking her time over it on purpose. It suited her mood to be perverse. He would just have to lump it.

She'd served two more tables when she noticed he'd moved his empty plate aside and was again looking pointedly towards her, between undisguised glances at his wristwatch. He didn't call her over, but his manner was enough to let her know he was waiting for the bill. Pretending to have only just noticed, Holly rounded the counter and walked slowly back to his table.

'Anything else I can get you?'

'No thanks. Just the bill. Or shall I go up to the counter and pay? That would be quickest, right?'

Wrong. Lloyd was in the kitchen, Jo nowhere to be seen.

'Up to you. It's me you get either way,' she said, before she relented and gave him as much of a smile as she could manage. He was a paying customer, after all. 'Stay there. I'll fetch it over.'

He was up and had his jacket on by the time she returned. He barely glanced at the bill, but fumbled in his pocket, brought out a ten-pound note and handed it to her. 'Keep the change.'

'But it's three pounds twenty. Hang on, I'll fetch it from the till.'

'No, really. Gotta go.'

'Well, thanks. I hope you get to where

you're going on time.'

'I better had.' Still no smile.

Seconds later, the door of The Ginger Cat closed with an unnecessarily heavy clunk.

'He had a face on him, didn't he?' said one of the women at a nearby table.

Holly rolled her eyes. 'Not one I want to see again in a hurry either.'

'Politeness costs nothing,' the second woman said, nodding vehemently over her cream-topped hot chocolate.

★   ★   ★

'I didn't think you were coming till next week,' Holly heard Carys say as she prepared their evening meal in the kitchen of Ashdown. The front door knocker had clattered, and Carys had gone to answer it. 'But as it's your house, we won't argue the point.'

'Sorry I didn't let you know,' came a male voice that sounded a tiny bit familiar. 'They asked me at the practice if I could spend a day there before I start officially. Get to know the staff and everything. I was going to drive back to London, but I changed my mind.'

'Haven't you got a key?'

'Somewhere. Couldn't seem to find it.'

The front door closed. Holly turned. The spoon she'd been stirring the risotto with leapt out of her hand and catapulted into the pan. It was him, the bloke from the café this morning.

To give him his due, he didn't break his stride but came right into the kitchen and held out a hand. 'Holly. Good to see you. Again.'

He smiled. Yep, worth the wait. Even so, she wasn't going to be bought that easily.

'Again? Do you two already know each other, or what?' Carys stepped between them, causing Isaac to pull back from the handshake before it had happened.

'Or what,' Holly said, keeping her

face rigid. 'You're Isaac then. How did you know my name? Did Carys's nan say?'

'Nope. She said there was someone else living here besides Carys, but she didn't give a name. It was on your badge, at The Ginger Cat.'

'I'm surprised you had time to notice.' Holly tossed her head, turned back to the cooker and fished the spoon out of the pan, trying not to flinch as her fingertips touched the hot rice.

Isaac's grey eyes widened, just perceptibly. 'Well I did. I was genuinely in a hurry to get to the medical centre, though. I didn't want to give the wrong impression by being ages late.'

'Why didn't you set out earlier, if it was that important?'

'Fair point.' He was right beside Holly now. She felt rather than saw the shrug. When she looked — she couldn't help looking — there was that smile again. 'As soon as I hit Sussex, my stomach told me I needed breakfast, and I remembered there was a place in the village.' His tone remained conversational and even. Clearly Holly's attempt to repay his shortness this morning wasn't making any impression. 'It's so long since I was down this way, I forgot you didn't have to drive through Charnley Acre to get on the road to Cliffhaven. I should have turned off before and saved myself time.'

'You definitely should.'

'Yeah, well . . . ' Isaac rubbed the top of his head, for the first time seeming slightly embarrassed.

'Is this a private party or can anyone join in?' Carys had obviously had enough of being the outsider in the conversation.

Holly explained, in as few words as possible, that she'd served Isaac in The Ginger Cat this morning.

'Good. Now you know which one of us is which, we can dispense with the introductions.' Carys peered into the pan. 'Is there enough risotto for three?'

'Oh no, don't worry about me. I'll

nip up to the high street and get some fish and chips.'

'No you won't,' Holly and Carys said in unison.

'The shop closed down months ago,' Holly said. 'There's a mobile chippy that parks by the post office, but that's only on Thursdays between five and six.' She picked up the bottle of white wine and sloshed some more into the pan of risotto. 'You're welcome to share this. There's plenty.' She frowned at the spoon she'd lifted out. 'It might be a bit gluey.'

Grouchy or not, Isaac was her live-in landlord. They had to get along, at least on some level.

He rubbed his hands together. 'The gluey-er the better.'

'All right, don't overdo it,' Carys said, fetching out another plate.

This was too much, Holly thought, glowering over her own plate once the three of them were sitting at the table. Okay, so he'd arrived a week early, but he would have got here eventually. A warning phone call would have been nice, though, even if he did own the place. This was their home as well, and Ashdown had a landline; he couldn't have forgotten his own number, surely. The fact that Isaac seemed a touch awkward — shy even — in his own home, eating at his own table, annoyed her rather than triggering any sympathy. He'd been sure enough of himself this morning when he'd been ordering her about in The Ginger Cat.

Holly suppressed a sigh. Altogether too much. She hadn't been up for her shower yet, and had a greasy fringe and a face like a grilled tomato. She'd never felt less like making small talk, but luckily Carys nattered on in her usual fashion, covering the silences left by her and Isaac.

* * *

'So, what do we think?' Carys slid into Holly's room just as she was sinking into sleep and plonked herself down on the bed.

Holly sat up. 'Well, I know what I think, and it ain't pretty.'

'Oh, come on, Holl. He's fit, you have to agree.'

Holly sniffed. 'If that's your type. Anyway, *fit* doesn't make up for the way he treated me this morning, nor earlier tonight. *Fit* doesn't automatically impose a personality you'd want to spend a lot of time with.'

'Why? What happened earlier tonight? Where was I?'

Holly laughed, and immediately felt better. 'In front of the telly, I expect. Don't worry, you haven't missed much. Just his lordship coming in here and asking me if he could take some of our stuff out of the bathroom cabinet and put it on the windowsill so he could get his in.'

'Sounds reasonable enough.'

'Yeah, I suppose.' Holly plumped up the pillow behind her. 'It's not been the greatest of days and I'm knackered.'

Isaac's request had been perfectly reasonable, and he'd knocked on her door and apologised for disturbing her. He hadn't smiled at all, though. In fact, he'd had a face on him like he'd had this morning in the café, as if he wasn't really feeling the words that came out of his mouth. She'd wanted to say that if he didn't like sharing his house with strangers, he should have thought of that one heck of a lot sooner. She wasn't going to stay where she wasn't wanted, although she couldn't vouch for Carys.

'If he's going to be a misery-guts all the time, it's not going to be much fun, is it?'

Carys drew both legs up onto the bed, resting them alongside Holly and wiggling her toes inside multi-coloured stripy socks. 'Oh, he'll be all right, in time. We can knock the corners off, if we try.'

'I'm not sure I want to try.'

Carys looked at her. 'Holly, have you changed your mind about living here?

112

Do you wished you'd stayed at home after all?'

'No, of course not.' Holly shook her head, although right at this moment she'd give anything to be curled up in her own bed at Spindlewood, with Mum popping in to say goodnight and dish out a bit of TLC. 'Oh, take no notice of me. It's been that sort of day. I've felt like a piece of the proverbial from the off.'

Carys frowned. 'You're okay, though? Health-wise, I mean?'

'Apparently, I'm on tip-top form, and so is . . . '

She glanced downwards and sighed heavily. If only people didn't keep referring to it all the time, like being pregnant had altered who she was. But they were only concerned for her well-being. She smiled.

'You're looking out for me, I know. But you don't need to. I'm fine, honestly.'

'That's cool then. I won't ask when you're going to tell His Nibs that his tenants are about to multiply.'

'I think you just did, and the answer is, I'm not. Not until I totally have to. There's no point in inviting trouble.'

She'd been thinking about this, in a vague kind of way, since Isaac turned up earlier. It wasn't practical to keep herself covered up all the time, not at home, especially with summer coming.

Well, she'd think about it again tomorrow. Right now, her eyelids were losing the fight to stay up.

Carys said 'goodnight' softly and tiptoed from the room.

★ ★ ★

Holly didn't see Isaac the following morning. She wasn't due at The Ginger Cat until twelve. Carys had left early for her nine o'clock start, as she wanted to call at her nan's first, and Holly had stayed in bed. She didn't fancy confronting Isaac so early without Carys there as a buffer. She was lucky; the front door closed just after nine and she heard the engine of his Honda starting up. Jumping out of bed, much refreshed and feeling a lot better after a good night's sleep, she took a long, hot shower and looked forward to having the house to herself for the morning.

She'd checked her phone last night and again this morning, in case she'd missed another message from Lorcan. Nothing, thankfully. Hopefully he'd take the hint now and leave her alone. She'd left uni. What more did he need to know? Recalling his words in that last text, she realised it had been all about him. He was missing her. Was he forgiven? Nothing about how she was — not that he had any special reason to ask, it was true — but the focus had been all on himself and what he wanted. Well, Lorcan could whistle. And as for forgiveness, he had no right to expect that, not after what he'd done. Even if she went back to university — no, *when*, not *if* — she didn't need to have anything to do with him. He was studying Chemical

Engineering, not English, on a different part of the campus. His lodgings were nowhere near hers either, or at least they weren't at the time she'd left. She'd be safe among her own group of friends.

A wave of nostalgia washed over her for Beth, Ruomi, Erin, Amber — everyone; the shabby house that always smelt of chips, and the English course itself. She even missed the countless essays, and the late-night treks to the library to bag a dog-eared Kipling or Hemingway, or a vital tome on critical theory before anyone else got their hands on it. Which reminded her, she must keep up with her reading otherwise she'd be a dumb-brain before she got started again. Rather than slouching around the house all morning, she could walk up to Spindlewood and bring back some of her books. Exercise was good; the nurse at the clinic had made a point of that. Not that she didn't get enough of it waiting on tables at The Ginger Cat.

* ⋆ ⋆ ⋆

Holly was surprised to find her mother at home when she arrived at the house. As she'd walked up the steep drive, key in hand, she'd spotted Mum standing at the window in the turret room. Mum immediately saw her, gave a two-handed wave, and by the time Holly had reached the front door, it was open.

Greeted with a very enthusiastic hug which nearly knocked her off her feet, Holly stepped back and grinned questioningly at her mother.

'I was just thinking about you, and lo and behold, here you are!'

Mum's over-bright tone set off alarm bells. 'Yes, here I am.' Holly went along the hall to the kitchen. 'Why are you here, though? Why aren't you at work?'

'We haven't gone back yet. Honestly, the school holidays are endless! Not that I'm complaining, but I bet the parents are.' Laura automatically went to the sink and filled the kettle.

'Easter hols, oh yes. I should've

known.' Holly felt guilty. Already she'd lost track of Mum's life. Her school had longer holidays than most others, she remembered now. But she shouldn't need to remember; she should *know*. 'Sorry, Mum.'

'Don't be daft.' Laura laughed. It sounded like a knife scraping a plate. Holly felt the bite of anxiety. 'Why were you thinking about me, anyway?'

A small silence fell between them. They were getting good at that.

'Tea?' Laura said eventually, unhooking two mugs and dropping in the tea bags.

'Yes, please. I'm right off coffee.'

Mum finished making the tea and put the two mugs on the table before she spoke again. 'I was wondering if you'd had a change of heart, now that you're this far along.'

Holly didn't need to ask what this change of heart might involve; Mum's face held the answer. A direct gaze, challenging, but a shuffle of her feet, too, tempering the confrontation with a touch of remorse.

'I'm doing this on my own, Mum. Nothing's changed.'

'You still haven't told him, whoever he is?'

'No, and I never will, as I said before. I really don't want to go into the whys and wherefores. You'll have to trust that I've made the right decision. Not that there was a decision to make.'

Mum's eyebrows rose just perceptibly, but she didn't pursue it. Instead, she said, 'That isn't the only reason I was thinking about you, of course.'

'If thinking translates into worrying, and I bet it does, then please don't. It'll be all right. *I'll* be all right. We aren't living in Victorian times. My life's not ruined by being single and having a baby.'

'Of course it's not ruined. You're young, so young still, Holly, though I know you think you aren't. You've got your life ahead. It will just be a bit different from how you planned it, that's all. That's what I keep telling myself, anyway.'

'And it's true, Mum.' It wasn't quite true, especially the 'different' bit, but right now it was what Mum needed to hear.

'Actually, I came to collect some books. I'll go up and fetch them. Can I have a carrier bag?'

'Under the stairs. Same place as always.'

★ ★ ★

Later, as Holly walked along the high street to The Ginger Cat, having dropped the books off at home, she began to feel guilty about Mum. The feeling had become a big part of her thinking since she'd got herself into this situation, but now she worried that Laura was still harbouring certain expectations which Holly had no intention of fulfilling. At least, she didn't think she had. It might be time to talk to somebody — the right person. She'd looked it up online, read as much as there was to read; she knew roughly how it worked.

But there was still time. She hadn't even had her twenty-week scan yet. That wasn't until the end of May. Get over that hurdle, and then she'd deal with the other thing. She'd be clearer in her mind then, better able to convince the relevant people that she knew what she was doing.

Grinning across at Carys clearing tables at the far side, Holly went through to the back room, removed the grey sweatshirt, and quickly slipped her tabard over her head. Something was different. The pop fasteners each side did up really easily, with room to spare; there was no breathing in and straining required to make them meet. She examined them. The tabs had been extended with a piece of material in a toning colour carefully sewn on and the pop fasteners replaced on the ends. Holly glanced in the mirror. Jo had come into the room and was standing behind her.

She smiled. 'That better?'

Holly could only nod. She turned to face Jo, saw the softness in her eyes, the biting of her lower lip. Like Mum, Jo didn't know how to play this. So many people wanting to do the best for her, all trying to say and do the right thing and not knowing whether they were succeeding or not. So much confusion, and it was all her fault.

'Did Carys tell you?'

Jo shook her head. 'I have got eyes, Holly. Why didn't you say something, you goose? What did you think we were going to do? Chuck you out neck and crop?' She laughed. 'Goose. Neck and crop. What am I like?'

Holly laughed, too. 'I'm sorry. I should've told you, especially as you and Lloyd were so kind giving me a job when it should've gone to somebody more experienced, somebody who wasn't . . . ' She glanced down and pulled face. 'I was working up to telling you. I kept putting it off.'

'I guessed that.'

A small silence, then: 'What do you need me to do?' She wasn't talking about her duties this morning, and Jo knew it.

'One thing, that's all. If you're feeling ropey, tell me or Lloyd and take a break. That's it. Otherwise, carry on as normal. Okay?'

Normal. Jo made it sound attainable rather than a distant dream. 'Okay. Thank you.'

The oven timer pinged, and Jo returned to the kitchen. Holly was glad she and Lloyd knew, despite her not having told them. One less bridge to cross. Further down the line, things would be more complicated, but for now the coffee machines were working full pelt and the tables were filling up.

★   ★   ★

Holly met Isaac on the stairs as he was coming down and she was on her way up to her room. He stopped her with a light hand on her arm.

123

'Don't hide away up there. Come down and talk to me. Or sit with me without talking, if you like. I'm easy either way.'

He smiled. Something deep inside Holly quivered in response. 'I wasn't going to hide.' Her actual response came out unintentionally sharp and defensive. Isaac sounded entirely different from the morose version she'd got used to, and it wrong-footed her.

Carys had gone to the swimming pool at Cliffhaven for the evening session, so it was just the two of them. They'd eaten separately. He'd been in the kitchen with the door shut when she'd come home from work, and by the smells and sounds she could tell he was having dinner. She'd had a lie-down on her bed until she'd heard him come upstairs, then gone down and made her own meal. Sometimes they shared meals; other times, they catered for themselves. It was a haphazard system, but it had worked so far.

She shrugged as if it was all the same to her, and turned on the stairs.

The TV was already on, a nature programme about puffins. Isaac sat on the sofa, picked up the remote and turned the sound right down but didn't switch it off.

'I like what you've done in here.' He waved vaguely towards the grey and turquoise walls. 'It looks great.'

Just as well, Holly thought. *It's not going to get changed now.* And then she hauled back the thought. If he could make the effort, so could she.

'That's good. You said we could make improvements, so we thought we'd crack on.'

'Nice job. I'll give you the money for the paint and stuff when I've been to the cash point.'

'There's no need,' Holly said. 'We got everything cut-price, and we're getting the benefit, too.'

'I'll make a contribution. It's the least I can do.'

'Okay. Whatever.'

Silence fell, but it didn't feel awkward. Isaac's next words took her by surprise.

'I know I've been a grouch. We didn't have the best of starts, did we? My fault. Sorry about that.'

'It's fine. I haven't exactly been sweetness and light either. Call it quits, shall we?' She drew her feet up in the chair and began picking at a loose cotton on the hem of her jeans.

'You've been avoiding me. I can't say I blame you.'

He made it sound like a casual observation, not a criticism. Even so, Holly felt defensive again. 'I haven't been avoiding you. We've got our own lives, stuff to do. Ships in the night.'

It was true. Despite living in the same house, their paths hadn't naturally crossed much, with Holly's job, and being out with Carys or up at Spindlewood, and Isaac working what seemed like exceedingly long days down at Cliffhaven. It was also true that she'd welcomed the lack of contact.

'It's not what I'm like normally,' Isaac said, leaning forward, elbows on knees. 'I find it difficult meeting new people, handling new situations. It's a sort of anxiety thing.'

'Really?'

That was a confession and a half. She hadn't been expecting that, either.

'I'm better than I used to be, but there have been a lot of changes in my life recently and it's got to me.' He rolled his eyes and grinned in a way that told Holly he was sending himself up.

'Well, we are what we are.' That sounded vacuous. She smiled and raised her eyes to let him know she realised that. 'It must have been quite an upheaval, changing your job and leaving London for life in the sticks at the same time. Anyone would be apprehensive.'

Isaac seemed lost in thought for a moment. 'Upheaval?' He gave a kind of snort. 'You could say.'

It was almost as if he was talking to

himself. There was more to this than appeared on the surface, but whatever it was, she probably hadn't helped by being stand-offish. She should have been more sympathetic and tried to smooth the path for him when he'd first arrived. She had her own problems, more than enough to contend with. But he wasn't to know that, was he?

'When you say you find it difficult meeting new people, is it just the work thing or would you include me and Carys in that?'

'A bit. Okay, more than a bit. At work — at the practice — they might be new people, but they've all got a set role. I know where I fit in. Funnily enough, it felt weird coming home to Ashdown, like it wasn't really my house at all. I've shared places before, but in this case, I wasn't sure how to relate to the two of you, if you see what I mean.'

Holly considered this. 'I think so. It is a bit unusual, isn't it, having tenants already installed and you being the last to arrive? Actually, I meant to say, I am grateful to you for letting me move in, especially when you didn't know anything about me. It came at just the right time for me. Thank you.'

'It's cool. There's plenty of space for the three of us, and let's forget about the landlord-tenant thing, shall we? It's not relevant, only in a financial sense.'

'Suits me,' Holly said.

'I met Carys once when we were kids but not since, so in a way I knew nothing about her either, apart from what I knew through our extended family.'

Holly grinned. She was warming to Isaac more and more; his honesty about his anxieties had struck a chord. 'We're not too dreadful, me and Carys, though? I'd hate to think you were disappointed.'

'Oh no, I'm definitely not disappointed.'

Isaac gave her a look which made her break eye contact. She began to pick at the cotton on her jeans again. If he could be up front with her, she owed it to him to do the same. Neither of them spoke for a few minutes. Isaac looked at the TV screen, but she sensed he wasn't seeing puffins.

'Isaac, I've got something to tell you and I warn you now, you might not like it.'

He turned to look at her, not just his head, but his whole body. Attentive. She liked that. She liked a lot of things about him. She dismissed them.

'I'm pregnant.'

She watched his face closely. Yep, he was shocked, although he'd almost managed to hide it.

'Are you sure?'

She laughed.

He smiled. 'What've I said?'

'Nothing, you weren't to know. I've been sure since the beginning of January.'

She could almost see him doing the mental maths. 'You're about four months then? Blimey.'

'Yes. Blimey. And before you ask, there's no father. Or there is one, of course, but he's out of the picture. He doesn't know I'm pregnant.'

Again, she could almost see Isaac's brain processing this, wondering about the situation. He blinked twice before he said, 'That's your business, Holly. I wasn't going to ask.'

'But you're wondering. It's all right, everyone does. It's not because I don't know you that I can't explain it all right now. It's not personal. I haven't told anyone about that part of it.'

'No one? Not even Carys, or your mother?'

Holly shook her head. 'Not a soul.'

It sounded weird, even to her own ears, confessing that nobody in the world knew the whole story. Lorcan didn't know she was pregnant, but apart from Holly herself, he was the only one who knew the rest of the story. And that was how it would stay.

Isaac got up from the sofa. 'I bought a bottle of wine on the way home. Can I get you a glass?' He slapped his forehead. 'Of course, you can't, can you? You'll have to let me off saying stupid things while I get used to this.'

He was standing by her chair, his hand resting on the back of it. She smiled up at him. 'Take as long as you want. I also meant to say that I — *this* — won't make any problems here, in your house. You signed up for two lodgers, not three.'

He frowned. 'Why should it be a problem? Despite the earlier clues, I'm pretty easy-going, honestly.'

Holly laughed. 'I believe you. But believe me when I say there won't be anything to be easy-going about.'

She heard the conviction in her tone. It seemed to seal something inside her.

'Well, I don't really understand what you mean, but I guess there's reason in there somewhere.'

When Isaac had gone to the kitchen, Holly hauled the baggy grey sweatshirt over her head and dropped it onto the floor. She wouldn't be needing that again.

6

The end of April brought howling winds to tear the branches from the trees, and ferocious rainstorms which caused the drains in the high street to overflow, sending rivulets of water rushing along the gutters to drench the feet of passers-by. Parsley Street had so many puddles in its pitted surface that they were impossible to avoid, and in Ashdown's garden the daffodils bent and swayed in the mushy borders.

At Spindlewood, rainwater pooled at the bottom of the sloping drive, sending up great showers whenever anyone drove through. The wind whistled in the chimneys; a ghostly sound, Laura said, especially at night. Holly reiterated her plea that her mother ask Clayton to move in with her so she wouldn't be alone. But Mum just laughed. 'It would take more than a bit of wind to scare me into doing something I might regret.'

As May arrived, the winds suddenly dropped, the sky cleared, and the temperature rose so that it was more like high summer than late spring. Ashdown's garden was a tapestry of colour, most of which was down to Clayton's enthusiastic planting. True to her word, Emily had sent them her old garden table and chairs, which now stood on the narrow paved area outside the back door — it wasn't posh enough to be called a patio, according to Carys, anyway. The others laughed and wondered, in her presence, where she got some of her ideas from.

Holly spent much of her spare time in the garden, reading or just enjoying the welcome warmth of the sun. And thinking; she did a lot of that, too. There was much to think about, even more so when one afternoon, as she turned to the first chapter of *Middlemarch*, she felt the baby move. Her hand automatically flew to the spot where she'd felt the movement, checking, wondering if she'd imagined it. But no, there it was again; an unmistakeable, surprisingly strong, ripple beneath the firm flesh.

'It moved. The baby,' Holly said to Carys that evening, as the two of them strolled round to The Goose and Feather to sit in their garden as a change from their own.

'God, Holly! That's so exciting! Why didn't you say?' Carys stopped in her tracks.

'I just did.' Holly walked on faster, so that Carys had to hurry to catch up with her.

'How did it make you feel?' Carys said.

'Confused.'

'Really? Is that all?'

'Pretty much.' She'd felt a lot of things, things she wasn't about to own up to, but 'confused' was definitely on the list.

'Confused about what?'

Good question. Holly didn't answer.

135

She pushed through the side gate of the pub and made for an empty table.

'Can I have a feel when it happens again?' Carys said, all wide-eyed.

'If you must. Not if it's the middle of the night, though.'

'You could always knock on the wall.'

'Oh yes. Good idea.' Holly rolled her eyes.

Holly laughed, but she was thinking about her friend's apparent sleeplessness which she was fairly sure was continuing. Whenever she'd asked Carys if there was anything worrying her, she'd met with a surprised look and a flagrant denial.

As Carys came back with their drinks and two packets of salt-and-vinegar crisps, which Holly couldn't seem to get enough of these days, she had half a mind to quiz her again and see if she could get her to open up. But Carys was in high spirits, rattling on about some awful bloke who'd tried to touch her up in the swimming pool. She was making a huge joke of it, and Holly didn't want to bring her down by talking about serious stuff.

Later, they'd moved on to chatting about their respective home backgrounds, Carys making Holly laugh with anecdotes about some of the wacky guests — wacky, according to Carys — who'd stayed at the Welsh hotel her parents had run. Then suddenly she changed the subject.

'By the way, Nan wants to know if she can start knitting and what colours you want.'

Holly sighed. 'I haven't the foggiest.' Then, aware of how snippy and ungrateful that sounded, she said, 'Tell Nan thanks very much but I've not really thought about that yet. Maybe later, nearer the time.'

'It's unlucky to get too many baby things beforehand. Yes, I get it. Don't worry, I'll tell her to hang fire.'

Holly sighed again, but inwardly. Everybody 'got it'. Except that they didn't. They were second-guessing and getting it wrong most of the time.

Which wasn't their fault, of course.

Carys changed tack again. 'Did I tell you? There's this guy at the gym who keeps asking me to go on a date with him. He's called Nick.'

'Ooh, what's he like? Tell me all.' Holly drew on her bottle of orange and passion-fruit juice through a straw.

'Nothing to tell. I'm not going.'

'Why not? What's wrong with him?'

Carys was beautiful and kind and lively; she drew admiring glances wherever she went. It was a constant surprise to Holly that there was no boyfriend now, nor in the recent past, as far as she knew.

'There's nothing wrong with him, as far as I can tell, anyway. He's good-looking, single, nice to talk to and everything. I'm just better off on my own. Men can turn your life inside out.'

'As you know from experience?' Holly asked quietly, watching Carys's brow crease and her brown eyes darken, as if she was remembering something she'd rather not.

'Yep.'

'Want to tell me about it?'

Carys took a sip of her white wine. 'There was a management training course held in the conference room at our hotel. He was running it. That's how we met. I was stone in love with him, thought he was the one, you know? We were going to be together forever.' Carys laughed. 'If you think that doesn't sound like me, you're right. I value my freedom, I wasn't giving it up that easily. But stranger things have happened.'

'What went wrong?'

'Turns out he had commitment issues, serious ones. He reckoned that came as a surprise to him as well as me — as if. It's an old story. Dead boring, really.'

'What was his name?'

'Gareth.' Carys banged down her glass. 'He didn't want to finish with me, but he made it crystal clear it wasn't going anywhere.'

'So you ended it?'

'It was complicated. It ended itself, really.' Carys looked away, gazing across the pub garden. 'He made demands of me, unreasonable demands, and stupid me, I went along with it. And then, well . . . I thought I'd put it all behind me, but lately it's all started coming back.'

Holly wondered what these demands were, but it was clear from the closed-up look on Carys's face that she didn't want to be questioned. Everyone was entitled to have secrets. Some things were not for sharing, and nobody knew that better than Holly.

Carys wasn't as tough as she made out, was she? Holly didn't like to think of her being unhappy.

'Is that the reason you came back to Sussex?'

'He was moving on to deliver the training course somewhere else, but I needed to get away. There were so many reminders, of places we went to and things we did together, and everyone knew everyone else in our little seaside village. They all knew we'd been in one another's pockets.'

Holly smiled. 'Like Charnley Acre then. You exchanged one small community for another.'

Carys laughed. She sounded like her old self. 'I *know*. What am I like? I've got no history here, though. I can start with a clean slate. At least I thought I could . . . but it's fine. I'm good, and I love being back here and our house and everything.'

'It's not easy. Forgetting the bad stuff,' Holly said. 'It will get better with time, though.' She crossed her fingers beneath the table edge.

'Yeah.' Carys looked thoughtful, then she brightened. 'Course it will. Come on, honey, let's get home.'

★   ★   ★

Holly and Isaac spent more time in one another's company as the weeks went by. It wasn't by design, it just happened that way. Or so Holly kept telling herself. Carys was spending more time at the gym and swimming pool in Cliffhaven, often leaving not long after she got home from work. 'I've paid a shedload to join, so I might as well make full use of it.'

Holly and Isaac would stroll up to The Goose and Feather, or sit in the garden at home if it was a fine evening, or just chill out in front of a film. Holly felt a bit guilty about taking up so much of Isaac's free time, and said so. He seemed to have no idea what she was talking about.

One afternoon, she was leaving The Ginger Cat just after five when she found him standing outside the shop next door, obviously waiting for her.

'I got off work early, so I thought I'd come and meet you, walk you home, if that's okay?'

'Of course. Thanks. Not sure why, though. I'm a big girl now.' She glanced downwards at her burgeoning bump beneath the check-printed cotton of her dress and giggled. 'One hell of a lot bigger than I used to be.'

'It suits you.'

'And other clichés.' She laughed again, trying not to be as pleased about Isaac coming to meet her as she really was.

He laughed too, and put a guiding hand on her arm as they avoided the traffic to cross the high street. 'Yes, well, I haven't spent too much time around pregnant women. I don't know the form. It's true, though. You look stormingly healthy, which is good, of course.'

'I guess I do,' Holly said, thinking of the wan individual she'd been at the start.

★　★　★

Laura rang to invite Holly to Sunday lunch at Spindlewood.

'Can I bring Isaac?'

Carys was in Wales for the week, visiting her parents, and Holly didn't like the thought of Isaac being alone,

143

which was stupid, of course. He might appreciate having the house to himself for once, and it wasn't as if he was short of things to do or friends to be with.

'Yes, do,' Mum said. 'Clayton and Emily will be here.'

When the call had ended, Holly remembered Isaac's anxieties about meeting new people. He'd met her mother briefly once, but not the others. Great. Not only had she assumed he'd be happy to have Sunday lunch at Spindlewood, she'd ridden roughshod over his sensitivities.

She needn't have worried. 'Brilliant. Tell your mother thanks very much. Will it be a roast?'

Holly laughed. 'Yep, with all the trimmings. And if you're lucky, Mum's home-made apple pie for pud.' She could almost rely on that since it was Clayton's favourite.

It was a pleasant, relaxed occasion. Mum set the table in the dining room rather than the kitchen where they usually ate, because of the extra space, but other than that it was the same casual affair as all meals at Spindle-wood were, guests or not. Holly needn't have worried about Isaac. If he was at all anxious, he didn't show it. In fact, he talked as much as any of them, and it was obvious that everyone had taken to him, Mum especially, the way she laughed heartily at anything he said which was remotely funny.

There was a slightly tricky moment when Holly and Mum were alone in the kitchen after the meal.

'He's rather lovely, isn't he? You're lucky, Holly, to be house-sharing with somebody like him.'

Holly looked enquiringly at her mother and frowned.

'Well, he is!' Laura's eyes were wide with amusement. 'Nothing wrong with saying that, is there?'

'Suppose not.' Holly looked down at the water in the sink. Mum knew her too well. 'He's okay.' She shrugged.

'You asked him to Sunday lunch, so . . . '

Holly laughed. '*So*, don't read anything into it. We live together. He was at a loose end. Anyway, in case you'd forgotten . . . ' She pointed at her bump.

Mum smiled and shook her head. If it had been anyone other than her mother saying those things, she'd have been embarrassed. Quite why was anybody's guess. She'd become good mates with Isaac, the same as she was with Carys. It was natural, when they shared the same house.

They'd walked up to Spindlewood rather than using Isaac's car, and when they left they took the roundabout route back to the village — up Charnley Hill, then left at the signpost to follow the steep, downward path that ran alongside the woods.

'Terrific view from up here,' Isaac said as they stood at the top of the hill. 'Hey, look. Hang gliders!'

Holly smiled to herself. He sounded boyish in his obvious pleasure at the sight of the colourful arcs sailing out into the blue from a distant hill.

'There's a club if you fancy a go. Several, in fact.' She opened the gate by the signpost and went through.

'I might, one day. You never know.'

'You don't strike me as the sporty type.'

Holly fell into step beside him, even though the path was really only wide enough for one.

'I'm not, not like our gym-bunny Carys, anyway. I don't play rugby or any of that. I have skied a bit. I went with the school, aeons ago, then again when I was a student. And I've chucked myself off the Stratosphere Tower in Vegas. That was a laugh. I was attached to a wire, in case you were wondering.'

Holly gasped. 'Oh God, I couldn't do that. I hate heights.'

'We all have our fears and phobias.'

'We do.'

They walked on in friendly silence, Isaac falling behind Holly as they reached a particularly narrow bit of the path. She stopped to admire the bluebells stretching far into the depth of the woods until they were nothing but a misty purple haze.

'Aren't they incredible? Bluebells are my favourite flowers. The woods around here are full of them at this time of year.'

Isaac stopped, reaching into the undergrowth at the edge of the wood and plucking a single bluebell from its bed. He gave it to Holly.

'Yes, I know, it's a crime to pick them, but it's just one. Nobody's here to see.'

As she took the flower from Isaac, their hands brushed; a miniscule exchange of warmth that was both exciting and disconcerting.

'What am I meant to do with it?' She waved the bluebell by its spindly stalk, covering the moment with a jokey comment. 'It'll be dead by the time we get home.'

'Right now, it's very much alive.' He smiled. 'Enjoy it while you can.'

'You are funny.' She held the delicate

blossom to her face and sniffed it.

'Funny in a good way, I hope.'

'Don't fish.' She grinned. 'Yes, all right. In a good way.'

They'd switched places on the path and Isaac was now in front. Holly wished they were side by side. Her gaze was focussed on his back view — the confident stride, the slight tautness in his shoulders tempering the confidence with a dash of shyness. She held the bluebell carefully at waist level, the bluebell he'd picked for her because they were her favourites, and strongly suspected that she might be falling in love.

And what a disaster that would be.

★ ★ ★

Holly couldn't help feeling relieved that her twenty-week scan coincided with an Ofsted inspection at Mum's school, meaning there was no chance of her being able to take time out. Holly sensed her mother's disappointment but didn't try to change the scan date. She thought about asking Carys to drive her to the hospital, but that would have meant neither of them being on duty at The Ginger Cat, leaving Jo and Lloyd in the lurch. Again, not an option, so Holly didn't mention it to Carys. She'd be fine going down on the bus. She had all day, after all.

And then Isaac happened to see the appointment letter, which she'd stupidly left in the bathroom where she'd opened it.

'Would you like a lift?' he said, waving the letter as they met on the upstairs landing. 'Sorry, Holly, I wasn't prying, but it was on top of the cistern and I couldn't help but notice what it was. I can easily take the day off. I've got tons of time owing to me from working late.'

Holly took the letter, about to decline and thank him, when she realised how nicely uncomplicated going with Isaac would be. There was no possibility of him coming in with her, as Mum and

Carys would, and to tell the truth she was a little bit nervous about this scan, for a number of reasons. She thanked him graciously and said yes.

As she'd expected, Isaac didn't go near the scan unit. Instead, he sat in the Honda in the car park with a newspaper and a take-out coffee from the mobile unit. When she returned, he looked almost asleep, head back against the headrest, arms folded, eyes half-closed. But as she slid into the passenger seat, he sat up, fully alert.

'All go well?'

'Perfect.'

'That's good then.' He started the engine. 'Off we go.'

And that was that. Easy, just as she'd thought. She settled back in her seat, smiling to herself.

Isaac glanced at her, smiling too. 'Okay?'

'Yes. I'm just pleased it's over.' *And that you aren't giving me the third degree.*

Mum would want to know how it

went as soon as there was a chance for them to talk, Carys too, but that was fine. They cared about her, and were emotionally involved because of it. Mum especially.

There had been a sticky moment in the box-like cream-painted room when the image had appeared on the screen and the heartbeat picked up. Holly had turned her head to look and, unlike the last time, wondered if she would ever be able to tear her gaze away, especially when the baby kicked inside her. But she did look away, once she'd heard the sonographer's explanation of which part of the baby was where and the reassurances that all seemed well. She'd spoken to the baby too, inside her head, to say hello, and to give him, or her, her solemn promise that she would do her best to make sure he was cared for, always. Seeing her hands clenched by her sides, the sonographer had given her a reassuring smile but said nothing, sensing this wasn't the moment for chit-chat. Holly was grateful for her astuteness and sensitivity.

Another wobbly moment came when she was asked if she would like to know the baby's gender. There was no apparent surprise nor any kind of judgement when, after a rush of doubt she'd pushed firmly aside, she'd said no. Neither was there any untoward reaction when, as she was leaving, she'd summoned up the courage to ask the question that had been on her lips all the while. The unit staff were used to it all. There was nothing they hadn't heard or seen.

The fold-out white card she'd been handed was safely in her bag, with the information she'd asked for in discreet blue lettering and a map of the hospital on the back.

★　★　★

That evening, she was drying herself in her bedroom after a lovely long soak in the bath when her phone beeped, signalling a text. She glanced sideways at it and saw Lorcan's name. It seemed more ominous than before, as if somehow he knew what she'd been doing today, and that was before she'd even read it.

She sat down on the bed, pulling the towel around her, and opened the message.

I'm scared you hate me now. Did you leave uni because of me? Would ring but you might not answer, couldn't bear that. Can we talk. L. xxx

Despite the warm evening and the thickness of the fluffy towel, Holly shivered. Again, it was all about him, his needs, never hers. Would he ring her if she didn't reply? Apparently, he was thinking about it. To get another message when she'd convinced herself it was over was bad enough, but to hear his voice . . . Well, she didn't know how she would cope with that. Snuggling deeper into the towel, Holly pressed in a reply.

I don't hate you, but I've got nothing to say to you. I don't want to talk.

Lorcan, please just get on with your life and leave me to mine. H.

Mistake. As soon as she'd sent the text, she began to shiver uncontrollably. How stupid! Why hadn't she ignored his message, like she had the last one? Now she'd replied, he knew she'd received it and read it. And he knew she'd received the first one, too. A fragile but distinct line of communication had opened up between them.

A perfunctory tap on the door and Carys came in.

'What's the matter, Holls? You're as white as a sheet. You didn't have the bath water too hot, did you? That's not good for you, not in your condition.'

Lovely Carys! Holly had to laugh. As soon as she did, the shivers stopped and she felt better. She released her hair from its towelling band and shook it so that it fell about her shoulders.

'How do you know what's not good in my condition?'

A strange look appeared in Carys's eyes, making Holly wonder and worry for a moment. And then it was gone, and a familiar toss of the head and a grin appeared in its place.

'Common sense, of course.'

'It might have been the bath. I did feel a bit wobbly when I got out.' It was worth the white lie to stop Carys worrying about her unnecessarily.

She pulled on her knickers and threw off the towel, draping it on the bed so that it hid her phone. She didn't even want to look at it.

'There you are then. You should let me look after you more. And him. Our Isaac.' Carys thumbed over her shoulder and gave Holly a pointed look. 'He'd like nothing better than to take special care of you.'

Holly felt her cheeks heating up. 'Stop it.' The grin spread across her face; she couldn't prevent it.

'Ha! Knew it!' Carys dropped onto the end of the bed. 'You're as into him as he's into you. Figuratively speaking, that is.'

Holly's heart took a dive. If Carys

had noticed something between her and Isaac, that made it all the more real, at least from her side. But Carys had a vivid imagination which she used to full advantage. If she didn't have the facts, she made it up for the hell of it.

'We're just mates, you know that. Same as you and me, and you and him.'

'Whatever.' Carys was clearly unconvinced. This wouldn't be the last Holly heard about it.

Carys got off the bed and went to the door. 'Are you coming down in a minute? I've made brownies. They're in the oven as we speak.'

'God, yes. I'm starving.' Dinner seemed a long while back. The smell of baking had begun to drift up the stairs, chocolatey and divine.

When Carys had gone, Holly resisted the urge to get into her pyjamas. Instead, she dressed in leggings and a floaty primrose-yellow tunic. Standing in front of the mirror, she brushed her hair, tucking it behind her ears, then smoothed moisturizer over her face and applied lip gloss. It would come off with the brownies, but never mind.

As soon as she appeared in the living room, Isaac stood up. He was wearing a shirt she hadn't seen before, in a deep caramel colour that accentuated his light tan.

'I'm off out. Don't wait up.'

'Oh. Well, have a good time, then.'

'It's just people from work, a few drinks for somebody's birthday. The guy who does our finances. I'm only going along to be sociable.'

Why was he telling her that? She didn't need the details.

As the front door closed, disappointment and relief fought to gain control in Holly's mind. Relief won. Just.

7

May burned its way into June, the long blue days and scorching heat more akin to the Mediterranean than the south coast of England. The tourists came in polite good-natured hordes to wander along the high street, tiptoe into the church, and, most importantly for the traders of Charnley Acre, to spend money on postcards, curios and keepsakes in the little shops before splashing out on cream teas, lunches, and drinks in the pubs.

The Ginger Cat was busier than ever. Overhead, rotating fans kept the heat down, but Holly's forehead broke out in a sweat after about half an hour, her feet ached, and if she was working a full day, by lunchtime a vision of her bed with its cool sheets floated before her eyes like a mirage.

Jo and Lloyd were wonderful and

caring. They wanted her to cut her hours, and even suggested a small pay rise so that it wouldn't be too disastrous. Holly thanked them but said she would rather carry on as she was for as long as possible. She was young and strong; she wasn't about to give in to her physical discomfort that easily. And besides, she was only just over halfway through her pregnancy. She'd feel much better when this heatwave finished. Anyway, it wasn't fair on others if she didn't pull her weight.

Mum, of course, agreed with Jo and Lloyd, and said so. Frequently.

'Am I not allowed to care about my daughter?' Laura said one day, when she'd arrived unannounced to give Holly a lift the short distance home.

She'd said it with humour and a lift of her eyebrows, but Holly sensed her frustration.

'Of course you are, Mum. But I'm as healthy as they come, and I'm going to all my check-ups and everything.'

'Well, then,' Laura said with a heavy

sigh, 'you know what you're doing, I suppose. But if it's the money you're worried about, you really don't have to. I can help, and I want to. I won't see you go short.'

'I know, Mum, and thanks, but I'm doing okay.' They'd reached Ashdown. The house was quiet; nobody else was in. 'Coming in for a cup of tea?'

They took their tea out to the garden. Mum admired the tapestry of cottage-garden flowers that filled the borders, some of which had been there all along, hidden by weeds, while others came from seeds and cuttings provided by Clayton or purloined from Spindle-wood and Carys's nan's garden.

Holly hoped she might have escaped more baby talk. She was wrong.

'If you won't let me help you directly, you will let me buy the baby buggy, won't you? Have you had a look at which type you might want, or shall we go together, have a bit of a shop around?'

'It's unlucky to get things too soon,'

Holly said much too quickly.

Mum's face registered surprise. 'Being superstitious is all very well, Holly — though you never were before — but it's not exactly practical. The months will fly by, and before you know where you are, the baby will be here and it'll be all of a rush to get everything.' She hesitated, bringing her face a little nearer to Holly's. 'You aren't worried about the baby, are you? You seem very well, and he's moving around, isn't he? Or she — although I can't imagine it not being a boy, somehow. No idea why.'

'No, the baby's fine. It's not that.'

'Well, what is it then?'

Holly sighed. Her mother wasn't going to be fobbed off this time.

'It was Carys. She said something about it being unlucky and it stuck in my mind.'

'What did I say?' Carys had come out of the back door, carrying a can of Coke. They hadn't heard her.

Laura looked up at Carys. 'Hello,

love. Holly was saying you think it's unlucky to buy things for the baby too early.' She laughed and raised her eyes. 'She takes more notice of you than she does me.'

'I don't.' Holly felt defensive, ganged up on. She looked pointedly up at her friend.

'Yep, I did say that, didn't I?' Carys flashed a look back at Holly. 'Gawd knows where I got it from, but there you go.' She sucked on the straw sticking out of the Coke can. 'There's a mile of time before she's due anyway. It's cool.'

'You're right,' Laura said. 'There's plenty of time.' She patted Holly's arm. 'I'm sorry to keep on. It's your baby. It's not even as if you need a buggy for the first few weeks, at least. You could have one of those slings. That's what they have now, isn't it?' Then, seeing Holly's face, 'Sorry, sorry, I'm off again. I can't help being a bit excited, though.'

Holly said nothing. She just nodded,

then leaned over and kissed her mother on the cheek.

Laura smiled. 'What's that for?'

'Oh, you know.'

She would have to talk to Mum soon. Her plans couldn't be kept secret for much longer, and it was unfair to keep her mother in the dark. If only she knew the right words to say. Perhaps they'd give her some guidance on how to deal with your family and others close to you when she went to see the social worker.

★   ★   ★

My life is closing in around me, Holly thought as she leaned on her bedroom windowsill one evening after dinner, letting the air from the open window cool her skin. *I move in an eternal triangle between Ashdown, Spindlewood, and The Ginger Cat, with hardly a diversion.* She was being melodramatic, she knew that, but it suited her mood. She indulged it a bit longer, conjuring up a mental picture of Birmingham on a summer's night, the streets thronging, the clubs and bars pulsating with light and music and life. Did she miss all that? She couldn't be sure if *missing* was quite the right term. No, what she felt was a kind of reverse nostalgia for what might have been, and what, surely, was still to come.

On impulse, she drew back from the window, found her phone, and pressed on Bethany's name. A ring-tone, then voicemail. The same with Ruomi. She didn't try anyone else. With a sigh that felt suspiciously like self-pity — shame on her if it was! — Holly took up her position at the window again, and saw Isaac mooching up the garden, looking at his own phone. She'd thought he was out for the evening; she was sure she'd heard him leave earlier. But it was all right because Carys was in.

I love you, said Holly's inner voice, the one she tried to fight all the time, only it wasn't co-operating. *I am in love with you, and God help me.*

Isaac turned round by the old pear tree, spotted Holly, and smiled up at her, pushing his phone into the pocket of his jeans.

'Fancy the pub?'

'Does Carys want to?'

'No, she's going for a run. I passed on that, by the way.'

'Oh, I see. I'm second choice, am I?'

'Yep, bang on.' Isaac grinned. 'No, really. Shall we?'

Holly hesitated. 'Not right now, thanks. I've got stuff to do. You go, there's bound to be someone you know to have a pint with.'

There was nothing she'd like better than to sit in a corner of The Goose with Isaac and have his complete attention for a couple of hours, but it wasn't wise. Not wise at all. Her feelings for him would start to show if she wasn't careful. He cared for her, but in a friendly sort of way. They clicked. They liked each other a lot, and that was it.

Would she have it any other way? No,

166

of course not. Even if she wasn't having a baby, after Lorcan it would be a long time before she was ready to risk another relationship. Regretful though it was, she and Isaac belonged to another lifetime, if they belonged at all.

A tiny foot, or hand, softly punched her pliant flesh. Holly's hand automatically cradled her bump. Her feelings for Isaac weren't the only ones she must suppress.

★　★　★

'I'm going to find this place.' Isaac stabbed at a pictorial map of East and West Sussex which was on the back of a tourist brochure. 'Woods Mill. It's a nature reserve near Henfield. Anyone want to come?'

It was Sunday. All three of them had breakfasted together on bacon sandwiches made by Isaac, and now the day stretched luxuriously ahead.

'We went there once, years ago, when Dad was alive,' Holly said. 'It was this time of year, too, and there were millions of bluebells.' She smiled, remembering. 'No, it must have been earlier in the year we went. They'll be over now.'

'Looks a good place for a wander anyway,' Isaac said. 'You up for this, Carys?'

Holly looked at Carys, willing her to say yes. Holly wasn't going otherwise. She'd have to invent another plan for her day. It was getting very wearing, having to do that all the time. It was dishonest, too, which left a bitter taste. A matter of self-preservation, though.

'A nature reserve.' Carys put a finger to her chin, tilting her head to one side. 'The question is, can I stand the excitement?'

'It's been manic at the practice this week. I'm all for a bit of peace,' Isaac said. 'You don't have to come, does she, Holly?'

Holly looked at Isaac in surprise. He was acting as if she'd already agreed to go.

'She'll come. Won't you?' She widened her eyes, just enough for Carys to
notice. 'A country walk will do us all
good.'

'Go on then.' Carys got up from the
table and attacked the frying pan with a
wodge of kitchen paper. 'If it'll keep the
pair of you quiet.'

They were piling into Isaac's Honda,
Holly having bagged the back seat,
when Carys's phone rang.

'Hang about,' she said as Isaac
started the engine. 'It's Grandad. He's
fallen over the back step again and
done himself a damage — he's always
doing that, silly old sod. Nan says she
can manage, but I'd better go round
and see.' She opened the passenger
door. 'Sorry, guys. Have a nice day, and
don't get lost in the woods.'

'We could all go round there now,
couldn't we?' Holly said hurriedly. 'You
can check on your grandad, then if he's
okay we can go on to Woods Mill.'

'No, no, you go ahead. I'll jump in
my car and catch up with you later, if I

can get away. Bye!'

Carys bounced towards her car, giving them a wave that seemed a bit too merry for someone who was worried about a possibly injured grandparent.

'You and me then, kid.' Isaac smiled into the rear-view mirror at Holly and patted the empty passenger seat. 'Come in the front. I'm not a taxi.'

* * *

'I don't believe this.' Isaac peered up at the sky through a tangle of branches. 'The weather's breaking. Look at those black clouds.'

Holly looked up, too. As she did so, the first raindrops spattered the trees.

'Shame. Never mind.' She carried on walking across a little wooden bridge.

'Takes more than a drop of rain to faze you, doesn't it?' she heard as she reached the other side.

'It's only rain.'

'Do you want to carry on?'

'Of course.'

There were a number of other visitors to the nature reserve: couples, families with children, wandering along the winding paths as they followed the nature trail signs. The shouts of the children carried through the woodland. The bluebells were well and truly over, just clumps of dark strappy leaves remaining, but spindly pink foxgloves fringed the woods amid a frothy carpet of gloriously scented wild garlic.

The lakes were a surprise. Holly hadn't remembered them from before, but they must have been here. It often happened like that; she'd look back at things they'd done and places they'd visited when her father was alive, only to realise later that the memories were selective and parts of them had somehow got lost along the way, like the missing bits of a jigsaw puzzle. Was it do with grief for Dad, or just the passing of time? She was surely too young to become forgetful.

And then, as they emerged from a woodland path that was no more than a track wide enough for a rabbit, a string of ducks sailed towards the bank of the lake, and a memory slotted back into place. Dad had taken photos of the ducks; he'd been keen on wildlife. A couple of the photos were still pinned to the curved wall in the turret room at Spindlewood. She must remember to look next time she was there.

She felt a rush of sadness. Isaac immediately cast her an enquiring look. He didn't miss a thing.

'I was thinking about my dad, that's all. Come on, let's walk faster. This rain's getting harder.'

It wasn't easy to pick up their pace. Once they'd passed the lakes, the path coiled through tufty grassland with shrubs rather than trees. The surface was uneven and pitted with invisible dips. Isaac reached for Holly's hand at one point. He did it in a steadying kind of way, but something told her he'd have kept hold of her if she'd let him.

She pulled away gently and walked on in front. If it meant anything, she didn't want to know. She swerved away from the thought.

They'd come full circle, arriving back at the first wooden bridge. Here, the trees were thickest, the overhanging branches in full leaf providing some cover from the rain. They stood for a while, not speaking, watching the raindrops pitting the surface of the lake. The ducks had disappeared. There was no sound other than the faint pitter-patter of rain on leaves.

'Can I tell you something?'

Her sudden need to share came out of nowhere, pushing its way up from her core and demanding release. Like the process of giving birth itself. She didn't wait for his reply.

'I think I'm going to have the baby adopted.'

His head jerked round, mouth slightly open, eyes wide.

'You're shocked,' Holly said.

'Yes, but only because it wasn't what

173

I'd expected. Nothing against you, Holly. It's your life, your business. Only you can know what's best, for you, and him or her . . . Is it a boy or a girl?'

'I don't know.'

'Didn't they tell you when you went for the scan?'

'I didn't ask.'

'I thought they just told you anyway.'

'It doesn't work like that.'

'Right.' Isaac nodded, obviously not knowing what he was supposed to say. 'You said you *think* you're going to have the baby adopted?'

'I was a hundred percent sure. Well, ninety-nine point nine. But since the baby's been moving around more . . . I don't know, it's not as easy to stay in the same mindset. I only know I have to.' She sighed. 'That probably sounds heartless.'

'No, Holly.' Isaac gave a firm shake of his head. 'Believe me, it doesn't.'

Mindset. What sort of language was that to be using about your own child? It helped, though, using neutral terms;

helped to keep her emotions under control.

'The adoption's not definite then?'

There was an unmissable chime of hope in Isaac's voice, which was unexpected, and puzzling. He hardly knew her. He had no right to have an opinion on the subject. All the same, Holly's heart went out to him. She almost wished she hadn't told him.

'This is not just about me, it's about what's best for the baby. I know the sort of life I want my child to have, and I can't provide that.'

'How do you know?'

'Because I do.'

Silence fell. Holly sneaked a look at Isaac as he stared out across the lake. His face was still, too still. She could almost see the thought processes going on behind those calm grey eyes. Eventually he spoke.

'How did your mother take it?'

Holly looked straight ahead, biting her lip.

'Holly, am I the first person you've told?'

'Technically, no. I went to see the social worker attached to the maternity unit last week, so she knows, but nobody else.'

'I'm flattered. I think.'

'I'm sorry, I shouldn't have landed you with that.'

'Yes, you should, if it's helped.'

Holly sighed. 'I'm not sure it has, which makes me even more sorry I've burdened you with it.'

'Will you stop saying sorry? If anyone's carrying a burden, it's you. *I'm* sorry you're having to go through all this. I can only imagine how hard it is for you.'

Enough. She'd already cast a shadow over the day as it was. 'I'm fine, or I will be. It'll all work out in the end, because it has to. I will talk to Mum soon, though, and then I'll tell Carys.'

'What will Carys say?'

'You mean you already know what my mother will say.'

'I'm only guessing.'

Holly pulled a face. 'I think you guessed right. As for Carys, I've no idea, but I reckon she'll be on my side, whatever.'

'As I am.'

Holly smiled. 'Yes. Thank you.'

They'd forgotten about Carys catching up with them as they walked past the old mill that gave the place its name and Isaac unlocked the car — at least, Holly had forgotten. And then, as they drove out onto the road, she remembered and the penny dropped. Carys had had no intention of joining them, had she? The thing about needing to go and see her grandad had been a ruse to send the two of them off on their own.

Holly smothered a giggle. It was kind of funny, even though Carys had got it all wrong.

Isaac glanced at her. 'What?'

'Oh, nothing. I just thought of something I wanted to say to Carys.'

She would be saying something to her, too, as soon as she had the chance.

She could do without Carys's schoolgirl tricks.

'Let's find a pub,' she said. 'I'll treat you to lunch.'

'You can't afford it.'

'How d'you know what I can afford?'

'You're always moaning you're broke, that's how.'

'That could be a ploy to get you to lower the rent.'

'No chance.'

They were both laughing. This was banter, nothing more. Mates joshing with one another. And that was just the way she liked it.

⋆   ⋆   ⋆

Holly and Laura cried in one another's arms. Holly had been scared of telling Mum, knowing she'd be upset. Even so, she'd underestimated the amount of distress she'd caused her. Naïve of her, but this was new territory for both of them, a giant leap into the unknown. Nothing in life prepared you for moments like this.

On the drive home from Henfield, she'd decided she had to do this tonight. Had it been some kind of rehearsal, saying those words out loud to Isaac? Perhaps. Or perhaps by telling him first, she'd been testing her own reactions. Whatever, here they were.

Clayton stood in the kitchen doorway, one hand placed high on the door jamb. Holly glanced at him past her mother's shoulder, but his face was passive, impossible to read. He was, Holly deduced, waiting to see if he had a role to play in this.

Suddenly, Laura broke away from Holly and spun round on her heel before facing her again. Her mouth was a thin, straight line.

'No. I won't let you do this. You've no *idea* how big a deal this is, that's obvious. Your own child and you're thinking of letting him go!' Her arms were folded around herself. She shook her head. 'No. It's not happening. You're having a baby, he'll be your baby, and you'll do the right thing by him and bring him up. We will bring him up, together.'

Laura's blue-grey eyes were bright with tears but hardened now with anger.

'Mum, please don't . . . ' Holly stopped, not knowing what she'd been going to say.

Laura and Clayton had been eating off trays in the living room when she'd arrived. She hadn't meant to disturb their cosy Sunday night supper, but a warning phone call hadn't seemed an option either, not without giving something away in her voice before she was ready. She'd asked Isaac to drive her up to Spindlewood. She hadn't told him why she was coming; she hadn't needed to.

He'd asked if he should wait for her. It would have been a small comfort, a fragile safety net, knowing he was there outside in the Honda, ready to take her home. But she couldn't ask him to do that. She didn't deserve comfort, not tonight. Tonight wasn't about her, it was about Mum. About helping her to accept the decision she'd made without too much damage being done in the process.

She wasn't doing too well so far.

Clayton made a sudden move and came right into the kitchen. He put a hand on Laura's shoulder. Holly expected her mother to turn to him, but she shrugged him off, not unkindly.

'I'll clear the trays,' she said, making for the door.

'No, I'll do it.'

Clayton went out, obviously glad to have something to do. Laura followed, leaving Holly standing alone in the kitchen. It felt like a punishment.

After several long minutes, they both returned, each carrying a tray.

'Clayton suggested we put some space between us, you and me, Holly, and I think that's a good idea. I can't trust what I might say to you, not right now.'

'Mum, I need to try and explain

181

properly, make you see that I do know my own mind, and this is not just a knee-jerk reaction.'

There had been a point earlier when she'd believed she was getting through to her mother and she was at least some way towards understanding.

'I'm scared, Mum,' she'd said. 'Not of having the baby or anything like that, but of resenting him because I'm selfish enough to want the kind of life I'd planned for myself — the life *you'd* wanted for me. He doesn't deserve that. If I can't give him a hundred percent of me, as his mother, then I can't give him any of me. It wouldn't be fair.'

She'd said much more, of course, but that was the nub of the matter, her belief that her child would be far better off with a couple who needed and wanted a baby so much they were prepared to haul themselves through the adoption system to get one.

Laura had sat in the living room, hands in her lap, and looked at Holly with something that seemed to signal agreement. And then her expression had changed, and she'd got up and walked off to the kitchen. When Holly had followed, not knowing whether to or not, Mum had been facing the sink, holding onto its edge as if her legs would buckle under her if she didn't.

'Don't put this on me, Holly,' she'd said, turning as Holly entered the room. 'Of course I had hopes and dreams for you, but life doesn't always pan out the way you wanted it to. So what do you do? You adapt, that's what you do. You adapt, and find the good that comes out of it. *And* you take responsibility for your actions.'

Holly said nothing. Nothing she could say at this moment would be enough. She went to use the downstairs loo, taking her time over washing her hands and face, and when she came out, Mum was nowhere to be seen and Clayton was standing in the hall, swinging the keys of Laura's car in his hand.

'Your mum asked me to drive you

home.' He led the way to the front door, leaving Holly no option but to follow.

They were mostly silent on the short journey. As they entered the village, Holly said, 'Clayton, I *am* taking responsibility. Mum thinks I'm not but I am, only I'm doing it in a different way. *My* way.' She heard the faint ring of desperation in her own voice.

Clayton glanced at her, patting her knee in a fatherly way that made her want to start crying again.

'Let her come to you now, Holly.'

'You'll see she's all right, won't you?'

'Of course.'

★ ★ ★

Telling Carys should have been easier than telling her mother. It wasn't exactly harder — she'd already practised the words twice today, after all — but Carys's reaction was more of a surprise, and strangely confusing.

'So there won't be a baby coming

home to Ashdown.' Carys said this so quietly that Holly only just heard. It was almost as if she was talking to herself.

'Not as it stands, no. I'm sorry.'

Best not to mention that, if she chose to, she could look after the baby herself for up to six weeks. It wasn't going to happen. It would be hard enough handing him over to be taken to foster carers in the interim before the formal adoption process began. If she'd spent six weeks getting to know him first, her heart would be ripped to shreds. As would Mum's, and possibly Carys's.

They were in Carys's room. Rain lashed the window. The darkness beyond was complete in a way it never usually was in the middle of summer. Holly was sitting on an old pink Lloyd Loom chair, the curved back of which was strewn with clothes. Carys was perched on the wide windowsill, wearing frayed denim cut-offs and a black T-shirt with 'Don't clip my wings, I'm an angel in disguise' printed across the front.

'It's not me you need to say sorry to,' Carys said.

No, thought Holly. *It's everybody, including you, sweetheart.* She patted her bump.

'I'm not the first person to have their baby adopted. It's not exactly ground-breaking.'

'And that makes it okay, does it?' Carys's eyes glittered in the gloom. The only light in the room came from the dim bulb of the bedside lamp. '*Ground-breaking*? You're talking like it's some sort of business arrangement.'

'Well, maybe that's the only way I *can* talk about it right now.'

Holly looked down at her feet. It seemed like everyone was out to break down her defences, even Isaac — he hadn't approved of what she was doing either, she could tell. Right at this moment, they were doing a damn good job.

'Carys, it's my life, my choice.' She

said this to boost her own resolve as much as to persuade Carys.

'It's not just your life, Holly.' Carys nodded towards the bump.

And then her expression lightened, and she slid down from the windowsill and sat on the end of the bed.

'Hark at me! You're right, of course it's your decision. I'm sorry. I didn't mean to go off on one, only it was such a shock, that's all.'

'Isaac said that, too.'

'You told Isaac?' Carys's eyes were wide.

'Yes, today, while we were at Woods Mill. Which, incidentally, you'd have known if you'd bothered to come and find us.'

They both laughed. They were on safe ground at last. Safer, anyway.

'Yeah, well, sorry about that. Grandad was fine when I got there, but by the time I'd chatted, the time was getting on, so . . . ' She shrugged.

Holly raised her eyes. 'I don't need your pathetic excuses.'

'What you need,' Carys said, suddenly serious again, 'or rather, what I think you want, is for somebody to say, yes, Holly, adoption is the sensible thing to do. You go right ahead and don't look back. But I'm sorry, I can't say it. If you're determined, then fine. I'll still be your friend and support you, whatever happens, but I can't promise any more than that. I'm sorry.'

A silence, then Holly said, 'My mother's not speaking to me.'

'Oh, Holly.' Carys sounded genuinely appalled. 'She's lovely, your mum. I can't believe that.'

'Well, it's not quite like that. She said she wants to put some distance between us, while she thinks about it all, I suppose. She's in shock and she's hurt so I don't blame her, but I miss her, Carys. I miss her already and that's only since earlier this evening. What do I do?'

'Nothing. Wait for her to come to you.'

'That's what Clayton said.'

It was two o'clock in the morning and Holly still hadn't slept. Neither, judging by the repeated dull thuds coming through the wall, had Carys, but that was nothing new. Her reaction to the news about the adoption was a mystery. Holly had expected questions — was she absolutely certain? What happened if she changed her mind at the last minute? — the kind of questions Holly herself would be asking if it was the other way around. But Carys had seemed so very disapproving as well as shocked, and although she'd tried to hide it, she hadn't succeeded.

But how did she know what she'd do if it was happening to her? It didn't seem fair to Holly that the people closest to her, the only ones who knew, were so against her. It only went to show that when push came to shove, there was only one person you could rely on, and that was yourself.

Pulling herself up in the bed, she

reached for her phone, intending to reread Bethany's latest round of chatty texts for a spot of light relief, when she realised that Lorcan's last message was still there. She could have sworn she'd deleted it — she'd intended to — but clearly she hadn't. Her finger seemed to act of its own accord as it clicked on the message and re-read it, along with her stupid, mistaken reply.

She thought about today's revelations, first to Isaac, then Mum, then Carys. Not one of them had mentioned the baby's father. If there was going to be a time for the subject to be raised again, learning about the adoption would surely have been it. But it hadn't happened, as if Holly, in her refusal to talk about that side of things, had succeeded in wiping out all trace of Lorcan from her life. And yet here were his words, right in front of her. Highlighting the messages, she cleared them, but as she settled down to try and sleep, her mind was full of Lorcan Jones.

8

The Christmas before last, Holly had come home to Spindlewood in a flurry of excitement, partly because she adored Christmas almost as much as her mother did, but also because she and Lorcan had just spent two very special days together.

Her first term had ended, and she'd been expected home right away, but when she'd explained, Mum had been cool about her staying in Birmingham a little longer. A party, Holly had said, and it wasn't a lie. There had been an end-of-term party, not the usual sort with hundreds of people packed into somebody's student house, but a ticketed event at a proper venue in the city. Everyone was going, and she didn't want to miss out. Of course, she'd be going with Lorcan, which made it even more fun. Besides, she wasn't so secure

191

as not to be worried that he might cop off with another girl if she wasn't there.

Later, looking back, she'd realised how daft an idea that was, because even then, in the early days of their relationship, deep down she'd suspected that Lorcan was more in love with her than she was with him. She'd even go so far as to say he was slightly obsessed, but she loved him enough to make allowances.

The party had lasted until three in the morning, when she and Lorcan had walked all the way home to her house, holding hands and smiling at each other like a couple of teenagers, and then he'd left her and gone back to his shared flat. They weren't sleeping together then. He'd come back at eleven the next morning and they'd caught a bus back into the city where they'd simply wandered and drunk coffee and talked, and kissed at various chilly stopping-off points. They'd done the same the following day, and the day after that they'd clung to one another beneath the soaring atrium of New Street station until the announcement boards had them haring across the concourse in different directions.

Once she was home, Holly had been caught up in the festive whirlwind of decorations, present-buying, and baking, and the preparations for her mother's famous Christmas Eve party. It had helped to mask some of the loneliness she'd felt after leaving Lorcan to make his way back to Wales for his own family Christmas.

And then there'd been Saul Fielding. Saul had been working for Clayton at the time, and Mum had allowed them to set up their Christmas tree shop in the garden of Spindlewood. Saul had a bit of a thing for Holly; she'd known that since the autumn when she'd kind of implied the feeling was mutual. It had been fun flirting, and a bit more, with Saul, whom she'd known amongst the village set for yonks. She liked him as a friend and was attracted to him, no doubt about that, but it had come as a complete surprise to her that as soon as she saw him again those feelings returned. If she was in love with Lorcan, what was she doing liking somebody else?

In spite of it being Christmas and the holiday spirit prevailing, she'd behaved properly and kept Saul at arm's length. They'd hung out a bit, which was only natural and felt fine, but when he'd asked her out on a proper date she'd gently turned him down. She was seeing somebody else, she'd told him, somebody at uni. But even as she'd said it, she'd begun to wonder why she wasn't missing Lorcan quite as much as she should have been.

Her doubts about Lorcan during that holiday hadn't truly been about Saul; he'd been the catalyst, that was all. It had taken her a while to realise that, and to understand that her personal freedom at this stage of her life wasn't something she was prepared to give up. And that was what would have happened, had she carried on seeing

Lorcan exclusively.

But when she'd arrived back at the start of term, there he was, already waiting for her at the scruffy house in the scruffy Birmingham street, and she'd felt both claustrophobic and overwhelmed with love for him at the same time. They'd agreed not to buy one another Christmas presents — money was short, and they'd each be their present to one another, they'd said in a romantic moment — but Lorcan had brought her back a little doll dressed in traditional Welsh costume. A joke, he said, but Holly loved it.

They made love that night for the first time.

★ ★ ★

The rest of Holly's first year seemed to wing by in a matter of weeks rather than months. Her English course and the part-time supermarket job took up most of her time. Lorcan took up the rest. They'd become Holly-and-Lorcan, each recognised as one half of a couple all over campus. Lorcan wasn't on the same course as Holly, but she felt obliged to spend her lunch breaks with him if the times coincided, as well as her free evenings and weekends. And slowly, against her will, she began to resent his constant presence by her side.

Bethany and her other friends thought his devotion was sweet. And it was, she supposed. Lorcan, with his striking looks, his consistent A grades and all-round niceness, was popular, especially amongst the girls in their year. What did she have to complain about?

At the end of that first year, on the last day of exams, Holly told Lorcan they were finished. He cried. She cried. But she stayed firm. This was her one chance to fully experience life as a student and she had to make the most of it, otherwise she'd be doing herself a disservice. No, she didn't want to sleep with anyone else, that was nothing to do with it, she'd told him when he asked her, his eyes deeply questioning hers, if he wasn't satisfying her sexually. It didn't strike her as odd at the time that this was uppermost in Lorcan's mind. Later, yes, maybe, but not then.

She'd explained how she felt in as few words as possible; she owed it to him, and herself, not to string it out and make it more complicated or difficult than it needed to be. *I love you, but I don't want to be this settled so soon. I need to be free to explore other friendships, to come and go as I want to. And you should, too.* A shadow of disbelief and denial had passed over his face like a physical cloud. She'd witnessed it, but there was nothing she could about it.

He had to let her go; she'd given him no choice.

9

Holly was so pleased to see her mother sitting at a table in The Ginger Cat on Saturday morning and smiling across at her rather shamefacedly, she could have cried. She held on to the counter for a moment, breathing deeply.

'What is it, lovely?' Jo was there, her eyes all concern. 'Don't you feel well?'

'I'm fine. My mum's come in. I haven't seen her or spoken to her all week because of something I told her that upset her.'

'Oh no, you don't want to go falling out with your mum. I bet it's all over nothing at all!'

Nothing at all. Holly wished that were true.

Not quite, she told Jo, but that was all. She needed to tell her about the adoption at some point. Well, not needed to exactly, but she wanted to, otherwise nothing about the coming weeks would make any sense. It would be like living a lie, and Jo and Lloyd deserved better. But for now, making it up with Mum was her priority.

'Go on, then. Take a break.' Jo smiled encouragingly.

Holly rounded the counter and went across to join Mum at her table. After a few minutes, Jo brought Laura the coffee she'd asked for, peppermint tea for Holly — she'd been drinking it to help with heartburn — and two rounds of buttered fruit toast.

'All on the house,' Jo said, beaming at the pair of them.

And then she and Mum joshed a bit about Holly needing building up, hence the toast. A spot of nonsense, but Mum visibly relaxed, and Holly's heart swerved when she realised her mother had been nervous about coming to see her.

When Jo had left them, they both spoke together.

'Mum, I never meant to . . . '

'Darling, I'm so sorry . . . '

They smiled at one another. Laura's eyes were misty. She shook her head as if to clear them before setting down her mug with a business-like clunk and leaned in towards Holly, lowering her voice.

'So then, what do we need to do? About this adoption, I mean.'

Oh. Was it going to be that easy after all?

'You accept my decision then?'

'I wouldn't go that far, but I do understand why you think it's the right thing to do. I'm your mum, Holly, and I'll help you and support you every step of the way.'

'Really?'

'Of course.'

'Actually, there's nothing *to* do at the moment. I've been to see the social worker at the hospital. Her name's Veronica Hampson. She's really nice. Anyway, she's the one who'll put it all into play when the time comes.'

'And that's it? We do nothing

meanwhile? You don't sign papers or anything?'

'Nope, not yet.'

'Nothing's set in stone, then?'

Mum's gaze was on Holly; hopeful, questioning. Holly hesitated.

'Not officially, no. I have to go and see Veronica again at some point, for counselling and to answer some more questions and stuff, but I won't change my mind, Mum. I know you think I will, but I won't. I'm so sorry you're hurting over this, but there's nothing I can do about that.'

'Yes, it hurts, I can't pretend it doesn't. It hurts like hell. I wasn't going to say it, but this is my grandchild we're talking about. He's my flesh and blood as well as yours.'

Mum patted Holly's hand to take the sting out the words. All the same, her stomach turned inside out. She felt a series of butterfly movements deeper down, and then all was still.

'I know, Mum, and you will have grandchildren, one day, just not now.

This baby will have a good life with good people. I wouldn't be doing this if I thought otherwise.'

'Holly, you are a good person. He'll have all the good people he needs, right here.'

Holly didn't answer. Laura let the silence stretch between them. She cut a slice of fruit toast into half and ate it, then wiped her fingers on a napkin.

'I did a bit of research myself, as it happens. About adoption, I mean.'

Holly waited.

'It seems the father doesn't have to be consulted if he's not named on the birth certificate.'

'I found that out, too,' Holly said. 'Veronica told me.'

'And are you naming him? The father?'

'No, Mum.'

Laura held up her hands. 'Okay, I'm just checking nothing's changed there.'

'Yes. Sorry. I didn't mean to snap.' The tables were filling up. 'I need to get on.' She stood up. 'Will you come and see me again, soon? Or I'll come to you?'

'Oh, Holly.' Laura had an air of sad defeat about her. 'We'll see each other all the time from now on. I'm sorry I stayed away. I just didn't know how to . . . '

'It's fine.'

'Promise you'll talk to me in future. You don't need to go through all this on your own.'

Holly nodded.

'And *I* promise,' Laura continued, 'to listen and not foist my opinions on you. Only if you ask for them.' She gave a rueful smile.

Holly rounded the table and kissed her mother on the cheek. By the time she'd fetched a tray from behind the counter to clear the tables, the door of The Ginger Cat had clicked shut and Mum was out of sight.

★ ★ ★

The rest of June passed in a miasma of grey skies and sharp showers. All over

Charnley Acre, posters were up advertising the annual flower festival and summer fete to be held on the first Saturday of July. The likelihood of the weather cheering up for the event was being debated and pondered with varying degrees of optimism all over the village.

'Holly won't mind if it tips it down on the day,' Isaac said, peering out of the window at Ashdown one gloomy evening. He drew air quotes. *'It's only rain.'*

'When did she say that?' Carys uncurled her legs from beneath her and stretched out full length on the sofa.

'When we were at the nature reserve. It rained then as well.'

Holly looked up from the book she was reading and caught Isaac's eye just as he turned round. His total recall of her words was disconcerting, especially when she remembered what else she'd said that day.

'I am here, you know. Anyway, that was different. Lots of stuff will get spoiled if it rains.'

'What kind of stuff?'

'The parade,' Holly and Carys said together.

'Parade?'

'The Flower Queen rides in front on a decorated horse-drawn trap, and all the children are dressed up and walk behind.' Holly giggled. 'I was Flower Queen once, when I was about ten.'

'Were you? I don't remember.' Carys swivelled round on the sofa to look at Holly.

'Well I was. Then there's the folk band, and the stalls all along the high street. All outdoorsy things. Even the belly dancers perform outside, in the square by the war memorial.'

'You mean Morris dancers, right?' Isaac frowned.

'No, belly dancers,' Carys said. 'They have classes in the hall every Friday. It's great exercise. The over-sixties love it, and they're all shapes and sizes.'

'Over-*sixties*?'

'Yes, why not?' Holly said.

'No reason.' Isaac shrugged.

'If it rains,' Holly continued, 'everyone crams into the village hall. It happened one year, absolutely fell down. It was chaos.'

'Remind me to be somewhere else on the day,' Isaac said, putting his hands in the pockets of his jeans.

'Oh no, you have to come,' Carys said, sitting up. 'It's tradition. It brings the village together. It might be totally naff, which mostly it is, but that's sort of the point.'

'Is it?'

'Yeah.' Holly laughed. 'Naffness is compulsory if you live in this village.'

'Yes, well, it doesn't sound like my thing,' Isaac said.

Holly felt a rush of disappointment. She'd been looking forward to going to the festival with Isaac, and Carys. The whole village turned out for it. Mum and Clayton would be there, and Emily. Jo and Lloyd were having a stall selling cakes and other goodies from the café, and there would be flowers everywhere.

The village never looked prettier than on festival day. As the events drew to a close, most people migrated to The Goose and Feather to round off the day.

'Although . . . ' Isaac was looking closely at Holly. 'If it's tradition and you're going — both of you — I suppose I could give it a whirl.'

Holly shrugged, as if she didn't care either way. 'It's up to you.' She went back to her book.

After a minute, Isaac said he had some work to do, and went off to the dining room on the other side of the hall. They used it as a kind of office and den now. Isaac had his computer set up at one end of the refectory table — he always seemed to have an overspill of work to finish at home — and they'd acquired a second television, which sat on a shelf in the corner among piles of books, magazines, and general clutter belonging to everyone.

'He works too hard,' Holly said. 'He doesn't get paid to bring work home.'

'And you'd know,' Carys said.

'What's that supposed to mean?'

'It means, sunshine, that you and he are — ' Carys held up two crossed fingers ' — in each other's pockets.'

'I wouldn't put it quite like that. We talk a bit, it doesn't mean anything.'

Carys flopped back on the sofa, her dark hair fanning out over the cushion. 'So you say.'

⋆   ⋆   ⋆

It didn't rain on the day of the flower festival. A light breeze sent picturebook-white clouds chasing across a sapphire-blue sky, but the sun shone endlessly. All week, the residents of Charnley Acre had been hard at work decorating cottage walls, fences and shop fronts with flowers. Window-boxes and hanging baskets were refreshed and watered constantly, makeshift containers filled with flowers were haphazardly positioned in every nook or corner, and bunting crisscrossed the high street.

After the parade had passed by and disbanded, Holly and the others bumped into Laura and Clayton at the stall selling fudge, coconut ice and marshmallows.

'I must say you look almost as beautiful as your mother,' Clayton stage-whispered to Holly, hiding his face ostentatiously behind his hand.

'I'm glad you said *almost*,' Mum said, handing round a bag of fudge. 'You'd have been in big trouble otherwise.'

They all laughed.

'There's nothing to choose between them, I'd say,' Isaac said, his face turning a bit pink as Holly and Carys gave him amused looks.

'You've got the right idea,' Clayton said, winking at Isaac. 'Keep the compliments coming and you're onto a winner.'

'Shut up, Clayton,' Laura said good-naturedly, glancing at Holly.

'What about me?' Carys feigned an offended expression. 'It took me ages to get this crown thing to stay on, my hair's so slippy. I've got that many hairpins in, it's like having acupuncture on my skull.'

'Yep, you look gorgeous, too,' Isaac said.

'Oh, I know I do.'

Carys performed a twirl, comically holding out the legs of her orange shorts each side, as if they were a skirt. Her T-shirt was blue with a single flower motif and silver lettering. 'Bloomin' marvellous,' it said.

Holly, Carys, and Laura were all wearing circlets of flowers on their heads, as were the rest of the Charnley Acre females — another festival tradition. Holly and Carys had plundered the garden first thing this morning, and spent an absolute age at the kitchen table trying to fix daisies, pinks, cornflowers and assorted greenery to florists' wire. Holly had taken her crown upstairs to fix on in her bedroom. She'd put on a sleeveless dress patterned all over with tiny multicoloured flowers on a black background. It was short, falling to mid-thigh, but her legs felt cool and the floral pattern helped to minimise her bulbous stomach. Smoothing on caramel-tinted lip gloss, she'd smiled at herself in the mirror, pleased at the overall result. The flower crown wouldn't stay straight, but you couldn't have everything.

Isaac had just come out of his room as Holly came out of hers.

'Wow,' he said, performing a little double-take on the landing. 'You look lovely.'

Flattered, but trying not to show it, Holly automatically ran her hand over her bump. 'Don't know about that.'

'No, honestly, you do.' His expression had been intense, as if it was important to him that she took the compliment seriously.

'Well, thanks,' Holly had said. She'd had no trouble meeting his gaze.

The moment had lasted longer than it should, but there'd been no awkward-ness about it. Holly recalled it now, and by the way Isaac glanced at her then down at his feet, she wouldn't have been surprised if he was remembering it, too.

'Hey! I've been looking for you lot.'

Emily arrived, towing by the hand a lean-faced man wearing expensive smart-casual clothes carefully chosen for the occasion. As far as Holly could tell, it was the same man they'd seen in the photos Emily had shown them, although he looked slightly older in the flesh. Not Emily's usual type, but that could be a good thing. Holly exchanged a look with Mum, who nodded, just perceptibly.

Emily introduced everyone. The man's name was Ed, and he was a dentist. A shy one, by the way he went pink as he nodded round the group and accepted a handshake from Clayton.

'I think,' Laura said quietly to Holly, as they all moved off slowly along the street, 'that he might be the one. She's been seeing him for two months now, and not one complaint have I heard!'

Holly laughed, and everyone turned to look at her. Leaving her mother's side, she darted in front to walk beside Carys.

'Is that Nick bloke still asking you out?'

'Why are you bringing that up? Oh, I get it. Everyone's loved up. Your mum and Clayton, and now Emily and her tooth guy. And there's you . . . '

'Don't say it. Please.'

'Okay. Sorry.' Carys glanced at Isaac, who was managing to riffle through the contents of the secondhand book stall while keeping a watch on Holly at the same time. 'It's pretty obvious, though. Look at him. He's only got eyes for you.'

'We weren't talking about me,' Holly said. 'So?'

'So nothing. Nada. Told you, I don't want to be with anyone.'

'Well, neither do I.'

'Right then. That's settled.'

Carys grinned, took Holly's arm, and they walked on in front.

The festival was winding down. The folk band had stopped playing and the hay bales, which had doubled as seats, were being loaded into a van. A crew of volunteers were filling sacks with speared litter and the stalls were packing up. Holly and Isaac sat on a bench outside the library, at the quieter end of the high street. They'd lost track of Mum and the others a while back. Carys had bumped into some mates and danced off with them, telling Holly she'd be back in a minute. That was an hour ago.

'The belly-dancers were well-rehearsed,' Isaac remarked, stretching his legs out in front of him.

Holly laughed. 'Which, roughly translated, means you actually enjoyed watching them.'

'Yeah, well. They weren't all over sixty, and those who might have been were pretty well-preserved.'

'You had a good time today, didn't

you? After all you said.'

'Yep. I surprised myself there. Good old Charnley Acre, eh?'

'Yeah. Good old Charnley Acre.'

The breeze had dropped; the air was warm and still. Beyond the roof-tops of the village, the sky above the distant Downs glowed rosy pink and gold. Holly slid down on the bench and tilted her head back against the hard edge of the backrest.

'I could drop off to sleep now, right here. I don't care how uncomfortable it is.'

'My mother says I could sleep on a washing line,' Isaac said. 'Luckily I haven't had to try it out.'

'You don't say much about your parents. What are they like?'

'Individually, fine. Together, a total car crash. They divorced when I was ten. Mum's still in Essex, where I grew up. Dad's in Perth. Perth, Australia, that is. With his new wife.'

'That must be hard, having him so far away.'

'Not as hard as having your dad die.'

'True.' Holly nodded, then, 'Are they wealthy, your parents?'

'What makes you say that?'

'The house. Ashdown. It's not exactly a cheap area. Oh no, that was intrusive. Sorry.'

Isaac smiled. 'You're curious. I would be, too. I wouldn't call them wealthy, but yes, they did help, my father especially. He gave me a lump sum towards the deposit and the rest I saved. I do have a mortgage but not a huge one. At first, I thought it was guilt money with Dad, but I soon stopped. He wanted to help me on my way and he had the means to do it. Simple as that.'

Isaac looked for the best in everybody, Holly was beginning to understand that. She had to try hard to resist the urge to hug him.

'When did you last see your dad?'

'He came over a couple of years back. He said he'd send me the fare if I wanted to go out there. Not that I would. Take the money, I mean. I can pay my own way.'

'You should go.'

'I will, one day. I was going last year, but certain things got in the way and I wasn't in the mood, funnily enough.'

'What things? God, I'm being nosey again, aren't I?'

'It's fine. You can ask me anything you want and I'll tell you. But for now, that one's best left alone. Why spoil a perfect day?'

Perfect day. It had been, hadn't it? She wished she hadn't asked that question, though. She didn't like to think of Isaac being troubled by whatever had gone on in the past, but when she looked at him, he seemed contented enough.

She levered herself up from the bench. 'Shall we go? The pub'll be filling up by now.'

The Goose and Feather was heaving with revellers. Glancing in at the door, it was obvious there wasn't a seat to be had, and the garden at the back was the same.

'D'you fancy this?' Isaac cast her a doubtful look.

'No, not really. I'm a bit done in for partying, and I'm starving. It'll take ages to get any food served up.'

'Well, then.' Isaac stood back from the open door. 'Can I suggest an alternative?'

'What's that?'

'We go home and I'll make us some supper. As long as it's pasta, because I don't think my repertoire will stretch further than that tonight.'

* * *

When Holly came downstairs after taking ten minutes to freshen up, remove the floral crown with its fast-dropping petals, and brush her hair, she was surprised to find the back door open and the garden table on the patio laid for two, with napkins folded into triangles. She hadn't even known they had napkins. Isaac had put cushions on the chairs and set the stub of a red candle in a tumbler in the centre of the table. He smiled as he saw her arrive.

'If you don't think it's warm enough to eat out here, we don't have to. It was just an idea.'

'No, it's fine. It looks very . . . '

'Silly?'

'I was going to say holiday-ish.'

The word came from nowhere, replacing the one she couldn't say out loud. How ridiculous and embarrassing it would have been if she'd said the set-up he'd created looked romantic. As if that was his intention.

'Holiday-ish?' He grinned.

'Yes, you know. Eating al fresco is what you do on holiday.'

'It's been a kind of holiday, the festival.'

'It has, hasn't it? Can I do anything in the kitchen?'

'No. You sit there and I'll bring you a drink. Sicilian lemonade okay?'

'Perfect.'

Holly sat, and moments later Isaac reappeared with two large wine glasses, both containing lemonade clinking with ice cubes.

'Oh, have a proper drink, Isaac. You don't have to go without on my account.'

'I might do later. For now, I'd rather keep you company.'

Holly sipped her lemonade and listened to the splash of water, the low clang of the pan colliding with the hob, the cupboard doors opening and closing. How was she supposed to keep her emotions from spilling everywhere and scaring the living daylights out of Isaac, and herself, when this cosy set-up had all the markers of a date? She gave her head a little shake, trying to force some sense into it. She was six months pregnant and tired after a long day. He was looking after her, that was all.

For a wild moment, her mind flipped forward. How would it be after she'd had the baby? Would she still have the same feelings for him when her body, and her brain, were back to normal? And how would he feel about her? What would she be to him? Housemate? Friend? Or more? Her pulse quickened with sudden longing.

He was in the kitchen doorway, speaking to her.

'What did you say? Sorry, I was miles away.' She held a hand to her face to disguise whatever he might read there.

'I was going to do the pasta with mushrooms, bacon, and cream. Is that okay? Not too rich or anything?'

'Oh no, I can hardly wait. Bring it on!'

Isaac was laughing as he retreated into kitchen.

★ ★ ★

It was dark now. In the borders, the white stars of daisies glowed. Floral scents filled the air. The empty pasta bowls and glasses stood on the table between them, along with three peach stones, one Isaac's and two Holly's. The candle had expired and collapsed into a wax pellet in the bottom of the tumbler.

Holly yawned, then gave a little shiver.

'We should go in. You're cold.'

It was the first either of them had spoken in a while; they'd been content to sit, each embroiled in their own thoughts.

'A bit. Let's not go in yet, though. It's so lovely out here.'

Isaac was up and heading indoors. He came straight back with a khaki Hollister hoodie. 'Put this on.'

'I might stretch it.'

'No you won't.'

Zipped up, the hoodie fitted snugly over her bump, her hands half-disappearing into the sleeves. It smelt faintly woody, like the stuff he used in the bathroom. Wearing something of Isaac's felt alien and intimate at the same time. The light from the open kitchen door carved shadows into his face and made his eyes shine. He was watching her while pretending he wasn't.

'Why are you doing this? Cooking me supper, lending me your hoodie, being stuck here with me on a Saturday night when you could be partying at The Goose or out with your mates?' Her voice floated lazily on the scented air, without much intent.

'Are you really asking me that or just wondering out loud?'

She laughed. 'The second.' *Shut up, Holly.*

A gentle roll, a soft punch, deep inside. 'Thanks for the reminder,' she whispered.

'What reminder?' Isaac leaned into the table.

'Oh. No. Not you.'

She should go indoors now, before she said anything else she'd regret. Pity to waste what was left of the beautiful summer evening, though. Besides, she felt too lazy to move.

Isaac went indoors again and returned with a bottle of lager. He took a swig. 'Can I get you anything?'

'No, I'm good, thanks.'

He sat down again. He was still doing that watching thing. She wished he wouldn't.

'I had an idea,' he said after a moment. 'About the house. But I guess it's irrelevant now.'

'No, go on. Tell me.'

'Well, I was in the dining room one day, at the table . . . '

'Working.'

'Yes, on the computer, and I thought what a waste of that big room, and wouldn't it make a great playroom if the table was gone. We hardly ever watch the telly in there. Or, I could move my stuff in and make it my bedroom, then my room could be a nursery. The attic wouldn't work. I took a look up there and there's not enough light, not without putting another window in.'

Holly had been lounging in her seat. Now she sat bolt upright.

'Hang on, Isaac. You were making

plans to turn the house around without saying a word to me?'

'That was *then*. Before I knew. Of course I would have consulted you. I nearly did at the time, when I had the idea, but Carys said not to. She said you were rather sensitive about the whole thing.'

'Oh, you discussed me with Carys, then?' She couldn't help the accusatory tone. Why did everyone think they had the right to interfere in her life?

'No; it was just an idea which I happened to mention to Carys in passing, that's all. Look, Holly, I'm sorry. I don't know why I mentioned it, because none of that matters any more.' He held up his hands. 'It's done. Over.'

Holly looked at Isaac, appalled at what she was hearing. It wasn't the actual words — although why he had to bring all that up about the house was beyond her — but more the way he'd spoken them, with a kind of sorrowful resignation.

'You're trying to pressure me into not

going ahead with the adoption. That's why you said it.' She pointed a finger. 'Carys does it, too. She doesn't actually say anything, but it's the *way* she doesn't. As for my mother, I see it in her eyes every time she looks at me.'

Holly stood up and pushed herself away from the table. The chair toppled backwards, clattering onto the flagstones. She fixed her gaze on Isaac. 'What the *hell* has it got to do with you, anyway?'

She slammed into the kitchen and stormed off upstairs.

10

Holly crept downstairs before seven the next morning. She'd slept fitfully, waking every hour or so to replay last evening in her head before thumping her pillow in a hot, destructive mess of anger and frustration. She'd jumped to conclusions, flung herself into defensive mode at the merest hint of criticism — as she'd seen it at the time — about her intention to have her baby adopted. She'd been horrible to Isaac and upset herself while she was about it, ruining what should have been the perfect end to a lovely day.

Sunday-morning silence pervaded the house. Two empty lager bottles stood on the kitchen counter in a beam of sunlight. Isaac's hoodie lay in a heap on the floor behind the door where she'd thrown it last night. She picked it up, holding it to her cheek before hanging it neatly over the back of a chair. She glanced up at the ceiling. No sounds. He must still be asleep, as was Carys — Holly had heard her come in just after midnight, creaking up the stairs with the deliberate tread of the moderately hammered.

Turning the key in the back door, quietly so as not to wake anyone, she opened the door and stepped onto the patio. The flagstones were rough and warm beneath her bare feet.

'Hello.'

Startled, she turned to see Isaac in the kitchen, a sheaf of Sunday papers under his arm. He was wearing a white T-shirt, faded bluejeans, and red trainers. The edges of his hair were damp.

'I didn't know anyone else was up,' Holly said.

'I've been to the paper shop.'

'So I see.'

He dropped the papers onto the table and went to the sink to fill the kettle. 'Tea?'

'Yes, please. I'll do it.'

She came back into the kitchen and reached into the cupboard for the mugs at the same time as Isaac reached for the tea bags. They bumped arms.

'Sorry,' he said.

Holly sighed. 'Oh God, *I'm* sorry. About last night.'

'It's okay. It was my fault as well, going on about reorganising the rooms.'

'As you are entitled to do. It is your house, even if it doesn't actually need reorganising. I was being prickly and oversensitive, as usual. I shouldn't have had a go at you, and I'm sorry.'

Isaac took the mugs from Holly's hands and set them down.

'Holly, what's happened to make you so untrusting, so unwilling to see the people who care about you as being on your side?'

She shrugged. Her defence mechanism awakened. She kicked it back into place.

'I wouldn't call it untrusting, exactly. You learn, though, don't you? You learn that people aren't always like you thought they were, and you don't much like the alternative version.'

The kettle boiled. Pleased to have something to do, Holly took over the tea-making. She handed Isaac his mug.

'Cheers. Do you want to expand on what you just said, or not right now?' He spoke gently, his eyes soft, fastened on hers.

For a moment she considered telling him the whole Lorcan story, and how it had all ended so badly. Well, not quite all — one good thing had come out of it. Something wonderful, in fact; she was about to make somebody's dream come true by giving them the family they longed for. Perhaps that should make up for everything else. Possibly it would, in time.

Isaac drank his tea and waited. If she could tell the story to anyone, it would be him. There was only one thing wrong with that. Lorcan wasn't the only one to have done wrong. She had, too. She'd made some bad decisions, the very worst, and right now she didn't want to sink even lower in Isaac's estimation by admitting to them. He clearly thought she was crazy to be giving up this baby. Perhaps if she told him, he would understand. He might even agree with her, and assure her that she'd made exactly the right decision.

Or perhaps he wouldn't. She couldn't risk another falling out. He meant too much to her.

Too much.

'Not right now. But thanks for not calling me all the names under the sun for wrecking yesterday.'

'It wasn't wrecked. I had a brilliant day. Let's just forget about the last few minutes of it, shall we?'

'I had a brilliant day, too. Thank you for my dinner.'

'You're very welcome.' He put his mug down on the table and held out his arms. 'Hug?'

Holly went to him. The bump got in the way of the hug, making it awkward, making them laugh.

'Are we friends again?' Isaac said.
'Friends.'

★ ★ ★

The university year ended, and Bethany came to stay. Jo and Lloyd gave Holly the week off from The Ginger Cat. Mum's school had broken up, and she drove Holly to Lewes station to meet her friend, then gave them lunch at Spindlewood.

Bethany fell in love with the house, as everyone did.

'You're *so* lucky to have grown up here, Holly. The turret is so romantic, like something out of a fairytale.'

They'd wandered out to the garden after they'd eaten, Bethany still holding her glass of wine.

Laura laughed. 'The leaks and draughts aren't that romantic. And the plumbing's starting to rattle.'

'Clayton fixes things, though,' Holly said.

'Who's Clayton?'

232

'Mum's boyfriend. I say he should move in, but for some weird reason Mum's keeping him at arm's length. *And* he runs a gardening business. I mean, what more could you want with all this lot to keep under control?'

'Oh Holly, change the record! Bethany, don't listen to her. It doesn't do to rush these things. You never know what the future might bring.'

'Hardly rushing, Mother.'

'He already does the garden anyway. He's coming over tomorrow to do the lawns, as it happens.'

Mum blushed a bit as she said that. Lawn-mowing was obviously not the highest thing on tomorrow's agenda. Holly pushed the thought away with a little shake of her head.

Bethany took her eyes off the turret. 'Is he fit, then, this Clayton?'

'Yep, for an old guy,' Holly said.

'In that case, I'm on your side, Holls.'

'Girls, honestly!' Mum was laughing as she set off along the path to the back door.

'Where do you live, Bethany?' Carys asked when they were sitting around in the living room at Ashdown after dinner.

Well, the three of them were. Isaac was away for the week, visiting his mother in Essex and catching up with old friends at the same time.

'North London.'

'And you're at Birmingham Uni. God, Charnley Acre must seem as quiet as the grave. What am I saying? It *is* as quiet as the grave!'

'I think it's gorgeous — the village, and the woods and hills around. Like something off that telly programme.'

'The difference being,' Holly said, 'we'll be escaping *from* the country, not to it. If we ever do.'

Bethany swivelled sideways in the armchair and swung her bare legs over the arm. 'Did you see it as an escape, getting into Birmingham?'

Holly thought for a moment. 'Not

234

going to Birmingham, no. It was the degree itself that was supposed to be my ticket out. Not that I don't love it here, but Charnley Acre can't be my forever-and-a-day.'

Carys was on it like a shot. 'Hang about, you said the degree *was* supposed to get you out of here? I thought you were heading back to uni at the first opportunity. Couldn't wait, you said.'

Carys and Bethany looked at each other before turning to look at Holly. Bethany knew about the adoption — Holly had passed on that piece of news soon after she'd arrived, feeling it best to get it out of the way. Out of everyone who knew, she'd seemed the least shocked. She'd also said she might do the same in that situation. Holly had almost dropped down and kissed her feet.

Then, as she'd listened to the campus gossip and the stories of working till four in the morning to hand in some essay or other by the deadline, the shockingly unfair off-piste exam questions, and living on jacket potatoes for a week when you'd run out of money again, it had dawned on her that somehow, without realising, she had stopped missing being a student, as if it had happened in another lifetime altogether.

'It's one option, going back to Birmingham. If they'll have me.'

The idea of returning to Plan A and finishing her degree after the birth had been the one thing that had seen her through. But the string had been severed, releasing Plan A skywards on a prevailing wind until it was nothing but a distant scrap above a blue horizon.

'Of course they'll have you back,' Bethany said, frowning. 'Why wouldn't they?'

Holly didn't reply. She thought of the coursework assignments she'd thrown together at the last minute, the assessments she'd failed and needed to repeat, and the missed appointments with her academic tutor where, presumably, she would have been called upon to account for her shortcomings. There'd been no point in attending. She wouldn't have been able to explain it, not in a rational way. Lorcan could be very persuasive. If she loved him, she would put him first. Was he not more important to her than revision sessions and essay deadlines? She did, and he was.

The irony was that Lorcan's studies seemed not to have suffered at all. He'd continued on an upward trajectory of academic success, regardless of the hours he spent with her. How he did that she had no idea. Well, she'd been the fool, hadn't she? In many more ways than one.

'You don't sound so sure about uni now,' Carys observed. 'What might you do instead?'

The question came casually enough but was heavy with unspoken meaning. Her discomfort must have shown on her face, because Carys was suddenly up and out of her seat without waiting for an answer.

'Why are we wasting time sitting about here, talking about boring life-plan stuff when there's serious drinking to be done? Serious lemonade-ing in your case.'

'Yeah.' Bethany stood up, too. 'Last one at the pub gets them in.'

Holly patted her bump. 'I've got no chance then.'

★ ★ ★

The week flew by. Holly had wondered how she was going to entertain Bethany — with Carys at work most of the time and Isaac away, their only means of transport was the hourly bus or the trains from Lewes. She needn't have worried; her friend wanted to see every bit of the village and its surroundings, and the best way to do that was to walk.

Despite her increasing girth, Holly still enjoyed walking, as long as it wasn't too fast. Most mornings, after a leisurely breakfast, they'd set off on meandering tours around the prettiest streets and lanes, chatting about everything under the sun as they went. More often than not, they'd end up at The Ginger Cat, where they'd eat poached eggs on toast, or deep wedges of quiche with salad, or chips if they were extra peckish, served by Carys with an exaggerated bow and flourish.

On Friday, the day before Bethany was due to head home to north London, they walked up Charnley Hill and turned down by the woods, following the circular route back to the village. Remembering following the same path with Isaac when they'd watched the hang gliders from the top of the hill, Holly felt an unaccountable wave of nostalgia, as if it was something that had happened a long time ago. She tried to work out why that should be. And then it came to her. That was the day when she'd first acknowledged her growing feelings for him. In her mind, she'd even used the 'L' word.

Even with Bethany here, she was missing him. Was he missing her? She doubted that very much. He was probably enjoying hectic reunion nights with his mates before crashing out and sleeping till midday. He'd hardly have time to give her a thought. Which was precisely the way it should be.

She'd slowed her pace while she turned all this over in her mind. Now she hurried to catch up with Bethany. Near the bottom of the path, where the ground levelled out, Bethany stopped beside a metal five-bar gate, beyond which was an undulating meadow, jewelled with wildflowers.

'Are we allowed to go in there?'

'Yes, but you can't cross it. You have to keep to the edge, where the public footpath runs.'

Bethany was already unlatching the gate. It squealed on unoiled hinges as they pushed it open between them, then clanked it shut again.

'Ooh, that's better.' Holly sank onto the tufty grass close to the boundary hedgerow. 'The hill took it out of me a bit.' She frowned. 'That's new. It didn't give me any trouble last week when I walked up to Mum's.'

'Sorry, Holls. I should've thought. I'm not used to . . . well, you know. You look really fit, though. Bursting with health.'

'No, just bursting.'

'Oh, d'you need to wee again? You could go behind the hedge, couldn't you? There's nobody about.'

Bethany's concern was so sweet, and so typical. Holly had forgotten what a good friend she was and how fond she was of her. Whatever happened about Birmingham and university, they'd always stay in touch.

'No, I'll be okay till we get home.' Then, after a moment, 'Beth, did you ever speak to Lorcan again, after that day he collared you outside the lecture theatre?'

Bethany didn't answer immediately. She drew her knees up, hugging them as she gazed across the meadow

towards the chequered sprawl of farm-
land beyond. Holly's breathing spiked.

'I didn't know whether to tell you
this or not.' Bethany looked at Holly.
'I've been worrying about it since I got
here.'

'Tell me what? Say it, Beth. You're
scaring me now.'

'Oh, no, don't be scared, it's not that
bad. You won't like it, though.' She gave
a rueful smile. 'Sorry, I should have told
you straight off, when it happened.'

'*Beth . . .* '

Bethany lowered her knees and
turned round to face Holly. 'Okay. Do
you remember a guy Amber was seeing,
around the time you left? A casual
thing; they weren't a proper item. Jason.
No, Jackson, that's it.'

'Vaguely. Why?'

'Well, a couple of months ago, this
guy told Amber he'd heard you'd left
uni because you were pregnant. He
asked her if it was true. It came right
out of the blue. He put her on the spot
and she wasn't ready for the question.'

Oh God. 'And she said yes?'

Bethany nodded. 'She never meant to but it just came out. She's dead sorry. She wanted to tell you herself, but I said I would, and it's taken me till now. I was wrong. I shouldn't have waited.'

'Never mind that. How did this Jackson know in the first place?'

'I don't know, Holls. Amber hadn't told anyone, nor had any of the girls, but somebody must have said something. One of the guys in our house, maybe. We kept it a secret from them, but perhaps one of them overheard something, or put two and two together. You know how it is. Somebody tells one person, and that person tells one other person . . . '

'I know.' Holly sighed. 'It's fine, I'm not that surprised. I don't blame anyone for letting the secret out, if it ever was a secret. Beth, are you telling me Lorcan knows as well?'

'I think he must do. Jackson's on the same course as Lorcan. We saw them together, in the refectory and around.

One night, they came out of the Union bar as Amber and I were walking past. Naturally, she stopped to talk to Jackson, and Lorcan acted all weird. He just stood there, staring at me. And then he nodded.'

'Nodded?'

'Yes, kind of slowly, and with a bit of a smile, like he was saying 'I know all about it.' That kind of a nod.'

'And that's it?'

'It's enough, isn't it?'

It was. Holly fell silent. She needed to regroup, inside her head. *Lorcan knows*. Had he known when he'd sent her that last text, the one she'd replied to? *Did you leave uni because of me?* he'd written. That could have meant anything. She decided she didn't want to know, that she wouldn't try and establish the dates. It made no difference either way.

Bethany pulled up a grass stalk and chewed the end. 'Holly, can I ask you something?'

'Yep?'

'Lorcan is the baby's father, isn't he?'

'Of course he is. What do you take me for?'

'Oh, I know. Only you never actually said.'

'No, I didn't, did I?'

She couldn't remember why that was now — that part of it seemed so long ago. It was probably because she was in denial at the time. Also, she may have thought that by not stating categorically who the father was, she was in some way protecting herself from him.

'Thanks for telling me,' Bethany said, her brown eyes softening. She leaned sideways and stretched a hand towards Holly's bump. 'Can I?'

Holly laughed. 'If you want.'

Bethany's hand landed lightly just above her belly button. The baby responded obligingly with a twist and a soft nudge, as if he knew about the attention he was getting — Holly thought of the baby as a boy now, probably because Mum did. Bethany smiled. The glazing of her eyes could have been caused by the strong sunlight. Holly didn't think so.

'Will you be able to . . . you know . . . when the time comes?'

'Give him up?' Holly flinched inwardly at her own words, but there was no use skirting round it. 'I'll have to, Beth. I really do.'

11

When she returned to Birmingham to begin her second year last September, Holly had found herself keeping watch for Lorcan on campus, in favourite haunts, and in the area where she lived. She hadn't heard from him all summer — not since the day she'd said goodbye to him. Ending their relationship had seemed almost too easy. Perhaps that was why she ducked out of sight whenever she caught a glimpse of somebody who looked vaguely like him.

Or maybe there was a different reason.

The guilt she'd felt after she'd ended it had faded; a busy, happy summer had seen to that. She and Mum had gone on holiday to a Majorcan villa with Mum's sister, Rachael, and her family; Holly had had a great time catching up with friends, and she'd spent several weeks as paid help at the children's nursery in the village. Most likely, she'd been wary of meeting Lorcan again because a part of her was still in love with him, but not enough to go back. If there was any going back. The reasons she'd given him for the split were still valid: she needed to work harder, without distraction, and being free and single seemed the best way to experience student life to the full.

As term got underway, she forgot to watch out for Lorcan, and it didn't enter her mind that it was strange she hadn't run into him. And then he'd appeared one Saturday morning in the supermarket where she worked, stepping right in front of her in the bread aisle as she was heading back to her checkout point after tea break.

She had more than one reason to be taken aback. It wasn't only the shock of seeing him which caused her feet to stall and her breath to squeeze back into her lungs. Two angry-looking crisscrossed scars ran down one side of his face from temple to chin, another drew a thin red line from eyelid to eyebrow, and he was leaning on a walking stick, the wire basket hanging awkwardly from the other hand.

'What happened to you?' were her first words when her initial shock had passed.

He smiled. Her heart would have given way, had her brain not got there first.

'I was in a car accident on the way back to uni. My father was driving, and we had a row with a council van. We'd only been on the road for ten minutes. Their driver's fault, not ours.'

'And your dad, is he okay?'

'Yep, he's fine. He got knocked about a bit, like me, but we were lucky. Could've been one hell of a lot worse if we'd been going faster. I've been at home recuperating, so I've got a load of coursework to catch up on.' He'd rolled his eyes. The scar below his eyebrow stretched and puckered. 'Bloody nuisance, but I'll get there.'

He'd asked how she was, whether she'd had a good summer. They'd chatted for a minute, then Holly had to get back to her till. It had been a relief to take her seat, key in her password and press the button to start the conveyor belt for the next shopper's items. The urge to reach out and touch the damaged side of his face had been almost overwhelming.

He'd suggested meeting up properly, asked her to ring if she'd like to do that. No pressure. If he hadn't been in that accident, she might not have given in to her mixed-up emotions. She might have said it was better they leave it, and she'd see him around. But she felt mean after she'd had to rush off like that, and she'd told him she'd think about it.

They met on the Tuesday evening of the following week, in the Union bar. It was Holly's choice, knowing she'd feel easier if there were other people around. Even so, she'd thought it best to be clear.

'This is just a catch-up as friends, right?' she'd said before they'd even sat down. It hadn't been a question.

'That's cool,' he'd said. 'I can buy you a drink, though, can't I? Lager okay?'

'Perfect. Thanks.'

They'd talked away, about the summer, their holidays, their worries and expectations for their respective second years, and Holly allowed herself to breathe out and relax. There were no tricky silences, no ambiguity. She bought the next round of drinks, and it felt as if she was out with a mate rather than a recent ex. They'd even sung along to one of the songs that was being played, one they both liked, and it was purely for fun, no side to it. Lorcan had moved on, that was obvious. Holly smiled into the mirror when she went to the ladies'.

He walked her home; his idea, although his lack of insistence made her agree readily. Besides, he lived closer now, having left his previous flat and moved into a tiny terraced house he shared with two others just a few streets away. She was living in the same student house as she had in her first year, with more or less the same group. One of the boys had left and another had moved in, but otherwise nothing had changed.

The October night was crisp and clear and starry. Lorcan had propped his walking stick against the railings while they chatted outside her house. He'd seemed in no hurry to leave. Then, as Holly was about to say goodbye, he'd made a sudden move towards her as if he was going to kiss her. She twisted away.

'No, Lorcan.'

He held up his hands, wobbling slightly without the aid of the walking stick. 'Sorry, sorry. Didn't mean to upset you.'

'It's okay. But I'm going in now.'

Unzipping her shoulder bag, she reached inside for her door keys, cursing herself for letting down her guard. When she looked up, he smiled, and the familiar rush of affection flooded in before she could push it back.

'Go on, Holly. A little goodnight kiss for old times' sake won't hurt, will it?'

He closed the space between them, only by one step, his eyes questioning. This time, Holly didn't move. She'd wanted that kiss. Unwise, contradictory, risky, but she'd wanted it. Even as her mouth met his, she'd known she was going to regret it. But what was life if you didn't live dangerously once in a while?

★   ★   ★

The following day, she'd spotted him sitting with a group on the far side of the refectory. She was with Bethany and Erin, about to join the lunch queue at the service counter. She'd thought he was far enough away not to notice her amongst the crowd, but he looked right at her, got up from his table, and pushed his way across. Bethany and Erin grinned, nudged Holly, and shuffled forward in the queue, leaving her with Lorcan.

'Holly, can I have a word?'

'What about?'

He'd tugged her lightly aside. 'I only wanted to say I enjoyed last night, and thanks.'

'I enjoyed it, too.' She'd smiled, keeping the moment light. 'I'll see you around, I expect.'

For a moment, his gaze had dropped. Disappointment showed in the stoop of his shoulders.

'Have a good term, Lorcan.' She touched him lightly on the arm and turned to slip back into the queue.

'Can I text you?'

'No, don't do that. As I said, I'll see you around.'

'Yep, you're right,' he'd said, pulling himself upright and brightening. 'Gotta look to the future. Can't go backwards. See you around.'

He melted away into the crowd.

★　★　★

The end of term, and Christmas, approached. In the intervening weeks, Holly had seen Lorcan a handful of times, and all had been well. They'd said 'hi', exchanged a friendly wave and a few words in passing. That was all. The season brought the usual round of parties. Stefan, the newest occupant of the house, was keen on Holly and made no secret of it, but he was good-humoured about her refusal to go out with him. She liked him a lot, but her plan to stay free and single took precedence. Besides, everybody knew it was a bad move to date somebody you house-shared with. It hardly ever ended well.

She did, however, go to a party with him. Bethany, Erin and Ruomi were going with boys they went out with on a casual basis, and it neatened up the group if she were go with someone, too. Stefan knew the score; he knew this was a one-time thing and seemed genuinely okay with that.

The party was in the road where Lorcan lived, and Holly wasn't surprised to see him there. He was with a pretty dark-haired petite girl Holly didn't recognise. He widened his eyes at Holly over the top of her head, and grinned. Holly grinned back, and apart from passing him in the basement kitchen doorway, she saw nothing of him for the rest of the evening. He wasn't around when she and her friends piled out of the house in the small hours, and she assumed he'd already left.

★   ★   ★

Christmas at home in Charnley Acre had been brilliant. Her mother's traditional Christmas Eve party had gone with a swing, as always. Christmas itself, with Gran, Aunt Rachael, Uncle Paul and the girls, plus Clayton, was lovely, and there'd been plenty of fun nights out in The Goose and Feather.

She'd relaxed and enjoyed herself that vacation, but with exams coming up and a pile of work to do beforehand, she'd been happy to head back to Birmingham straight after New Year, the week before term started. She'd scraped through her first year — she couldn't afford to mess this one up as well.

Lorcan had also returned early from his home in Wales. Holly had just arranged her laptop and books on the Victorian poets on the desk in front of the window when the doorbell rang. She bounced downstairs, expecting it to be Bethany or one of the others. Flinging the door open, letting in a blast of freezing air, she found Lorcan on the step. It had begun to snow, a few light flakes. Some had fastened themselves to his hair and the shoulders of his black padded jacket.

'I thought it was you I saw coming out of the corner shop yesterday.'

He smiled. She shouldn't have been pleased to see him — everything pointed to the opposite — and yet, for some reason, she was. Even so, she didn't ask him in, not right away.

'You're back early, too, then.' She rolled her eyes. 'Too much work to do like me, I expect.'

An answering eye-roll. 'Tell me about it.'

'So . . . ?'

What did he want? She really needed to get on with her work, otherwise she might as well have stayed at home.

'I was passing the baker's, and these spoke to me.' He held up a paper bag. 'Chelsea buns. Remember when we talked about the food we liked, and these came pretty much top of the list? I got two. One's for you. I'm not that much of a gannet.'

'Well, I was working, but that's an offer I can't refuse.' She'd opened the door wider for Lorcan to enter.

The Chelsea buns were still faintly warm, deliciously squidgy, and sticky with sugar on top. They devoured them in the kitchen with mugs of tea. The house was quiet. Erin had also returned early from the Christmas holidays, but had a bad cold and was tucked up in bed in her room. One of the boys — not Stefan — was back, too, but had gone out. Sitting across the table from Lorcan, the skies through the window darkening by the minute, felt cosy and intimate. There was no reason why they shouldn't be friends, was there? It wasn't as if they'd had a massive falling out or anything.

Lorcan didn't talk much; neither of them did. The silences were easy, comfortable. The kitchen was the warmest room in the house. Holly thought of her books waiting upstairs but didn't want to move.

'You've got sugar on your chin,' Lorcan observed.

'You've got sugar round your mouth.'

It may have been the word 'mouth' that changed the dynamic between them, she didn't know, but she found herself looking out of the misty window, unable to meet Lorcan's gaze.

'Holly . . . ' He shifted his chair so that he was closer to her side of the table.

'Mm?'

She managed to look at him, and at once they were kissing. Kisses that were sweet with sugar, fiery in their intensity. She had no idea how it happened. She only knew she'd wanted it to happen as much as he did.

'That was nice,' he'd said, when they broke apart, Holly first. 'Thank you.'

She'd laughed at his formality, gently making fun of him. And then they'd gone upstairs.

They'd been together in her bedroom numerous times, as they had in Lorcan's. It didn't necessarily mean anything. Bedrooms when you were in shared accommodation were places to hang out in private; they were not synonymous with sex. They may have transferred themselves to her room on that occasion because they'd heard Erin moving around overhead, she couldn't remember now, or whose idea it had been.

Once they were there, with the door closed, they sat on the edge of the bed, chatting about their respective Christmases. Holly had expected that soon they'd each say they had things to do, she'd thank him for the Chelsea buns, and Lorcan would leave. The next time she saw him would be in the street or on campus, when they'd acknowledge each other in a friendly way, as before, and move on, into their respective days.

Too late, she realised she hadn't factored into this scenario the power they had over each other. She'd overlooked the way her body responded to his, and when he kissed her again, the fire of their earlier kisses rushed back with a new urgency that refused to be repelled. He tugged her down onto the bed and the touching began, the pulling of clothes, skin on skin, and Holly was lost.

12

'I'm so glad you've cut your hours at the café,' Laura said as Holly opened the door of Ashdown to her one afternoon. 'Being on your feet all day isn't ideal, not now.' She gave Holly's bump a perfunctory pat.

'I know. I'm carrying on with three half days a week, though, plus the occasional Saturday. Honestly, Mum, I'm fine, don't worry. I'd go stir crazy if I had to sit around here all day.'

Laura smiled and went through to the living room. 'Yes, I know you would. How was your last check-up? All okay?'

'Yep, all in order. What've you got there?'

Holly eyed the brown paper carrier bag with a discreet logo as Mum put it down on the sofa.

'Now, don't go all funny on me,

Holly. It's just a few things for the baby, to start him off. You can't send him out into the world naked, can you?'

She laughed. It sounded strained, and a little bit desperate. Mixed emotions — old favourites now — swung through Holly's brain, robbing her of the power of speech.

'Come and sit down.' Mum did so herself and patted the sofa beside her. She seemed to be doing a lot of patting today. 'Have a look, tell me if you like them.'

Holly sat. Opening the bag, she peered inside, then looked up at her mother. Laura's eyes were full of sadness, love, and hope. Or was it despair?

What am I doing to you?

Mum was right, though. The baby would need things to tide him over directly after he was born, and afterwards, when he went to his foster carers. It was up to her to make sure he had them. Upstairs on the landing, in a drawer of the ugly Chinese chest that they hadn't got round to painting, were some packets of newborn-size dispos-able nappies, some wipes, a bib, two white sleepsuits, and a pack of extraor-dinarily tiny white cotton vests. There was also a small golden-furred teddy bear with velvet-lined ears and paws, and a rather earnest expression. She'd told nobody they were there.

Mum's bag contained three more sleepsuits — one white, one pale turquoise, and one soft yellow. They looked more expensive than the suits Holly had bought, and came on dinky little plastic hangers.

'Are they all right? We don't do the pink or blue thing, I know, but I thought it best to play safe.'

There were more things: a whisper-soft shawl in cream wool, a yellow cellular blanket edged in satin, a set of miniature socks, two silver-grey knitted jackets with hoods, and more vests.

Holly held the shawl to her cheek, swallowing back the knot in her throat. Then she smiled and packed everything back inside the bag, her movements brisk and efficient.

'Fantastic, Mum. Thanks ever so.'

Laura stood up. 'Right. Do I get a cup of tea or what?'

* * *

It was too chilly to sit out in the garden, and the clouds were building up. Holly told her mother to sit down again while she made the tea. She'd noticed there were more crinkles around Mum's eyes than usual, and she'd smothered a yawn earlier. Holly brought through a plate of The Ginger Cat's buttery shortbread triangles, given to her by Lloyd at the end of her shift yesterday, and set it down with the mugs of tea on the sixties retro coffee table — a new purchase from the second-hand shop in the high street.

'How was Gran?' Laura had spent last weekend in Hampshire, visiting her mother.

'Fighting fit, as usual. Her knees

aren't brilliant, but she doesn't complain. Not much, anyway.' Laura laughed. 'She would like to see you, though. She'd hoped I'd have brought you with me, but I explained you were working, and perhaps the journey might be a bit of a trial.'

'Thanks. Mum, how much does Gran know? And Auntie Rachael?'

It wasn't only her immediate circle who were interested in what was happening with her, she realised that. But it had seemed too much to deal with before, too many people's feelings to consider. Dad didn't have any close living relatives, but Mum's side knew Holly was pregnant. Mum had kept the news to herself until Holly was five months along, and then she'd told them. She'd had to, she'd said to Holly at the time; it wasn't fair to keep the people who loved her in the dark. She was right, of course.

Mum sighed. 'I couldn't do it. I couldn't tell Gran about the adoption. I'm sorry, I know I should have, and I will do . . . soon. But I couldn't find the words. Rachael knows, though. I told her on the phone the other week. She won't say anything to Gran. It's our news. Well, yours, I mean.'

'I don't mind you telling them, Mum. I know I shouldn't want to make this easier for myself but it's probably better coming from you.'

'I wouldn't say you're having an easy time of it, Holly. Far from it. If I could take the pain away from you, I would. You know that, don't you?'

Holly nodded. 'Maybe it *should* be me who tells Gran, though. I have to face up to this. It's my fault, I made this happen.'

Laura raised her eyebrows. 'Not entirely, Holly.'

'Yes, well.'

Holly looked down at the biscuit in her hand. Perhaps if she told her mother the full story, she would understand why she couldn't keep this child. But what would it solve? Confessing the truth would only add anger to Laura's list of negative emotions — anger on Holly's behalf. No. Perhaps one day in the future, when it was all over, she would. Not now.

She changed the subject, steering the chat towards Emily and her new man, the dentist called Ed. Barely suppressing a sigh, Mum went along with it.

★   ★   ★

That evening, while the others prepared dinner, Holly sat in her room and phoned her grandmother.

'I expect I've given you a shock,' Holly said after she'd explained, in the briefest possible terms, about her plan to have the baby adopted. 'I'm sorry, Gran.'

There'd been a short silence, then Gran's usual cheery voice trilled down the line. 'I'm not that easily shocked, lovey. I imagine you've had enough of the ifs and buts and whatnots from your mother, so we won't go into that.

Besides, it's not my place to pass judgment. But I will say this. It's your life, your decision, and I only hope and trust that it's the right one for you.' Another pause, then, 'Will that do? Have I passed?'

'Oh, Gran.' Holly didn't know whether to laugh or cry. Laughter won. 'It's not a test. But thank you. It'll do nicely.'

★   ★   ★

On Saturday, Isaac met Holly from work when she finished at five o'clock.

'I wondered,' he said as they crossed the road and made for the turning that led to Parsley Street, 'whether you'd noticed anything wrong with Carys.'

'Like what?'

'Nothing concrete. She seems a bit kind of faraway sometimes, locked in her own world, as if she's got something on her mind. I was going to ask her if she wanted to talk about anything, and then I thought it might be better coming from you.'

'She doesn't sleep very well,' Holly said. 'I asked her about that ages ago and she denied it, but I still hear her moving about in the night. Can't say I've noticed anything else.'

If Isaac was right and Carys did have worries, then shame on her for being so wrapped up in herself she hadn't noticed.

'I could have a word with her, but I wouldn't want her to think we've been talking about her behind her back. Anyway, it's not much to go on, is it?'

'S'pose not,' Isaac said as they turned the corner into Parsley Street. 'There was one thing, though. I said something about you and the pregnancy — nothing personal, just a mention in passing — and she went quiet. Walked away from me, actually.'

'Or maybe you just imagined that?'

'You're right, she's probably fine. I do have a habit of making it up as I go along.' Isaac gave a self-deprecating laugh.

'You're just . . . ' Holly began.

'Just what?'

She'd been going to say 'caring', which was exactly what Isaac was, but she'd only have embarrassed him.

'Oh, nothing, I don't know.' She pushed open the gate of Ashdown. 'It's good to be home. My feet are giving me hell. All I want now is a nice cup of tea and a long soak in the bath. With bubbles, if Carys hasn't used it all.'

Glancing at Isaac as they went in through the front door, she thought she saw the faintest sensation of colour in his cheeks, a little smile playing around the corners of his mouth. Had it been the mention of the bubble bath? Suddenly an image arose in her mind of Isaac himself, up to his chest in bubbles, his torso all gleaming wet. Now that would be something worth seeing. She quelled the image, fast.

Carys seemed her usual upbeat self when she came home from visiting her grandparents, as she'd had the day off from the café.

'I hung Nan's washing out for her, and what does she do?' Carys's laughter rang out in the kitchen as she peeled potatoes for mash. 'Tells me I've done it all wrong. Like, what does it matter which way up you hang a bloody pillowcase? They're the same all the way round. Oh no, the opening has to be at the bottom so the air can get inside.'

'Yep, that's grandmothers for you. Although I don't think mine gives a noodle about stuff like washing,' Holly said.

Isaac was frying sausages, big fat ones from the butcher's in the village. She wrinkled her nose up at the smell. She thought she'd got over the going-off food thing.

'I might turn vegetarian.' She peered over Isaac's shoulder at the frying pan.

'Not tonight you won't.' He flipped the sausages over, spattering fat. 'Not unless you want eggs. Or should I say an egg; there's only one left.'

'I only said might.'

She ate three sausages and thoroughly enjoyed them, to the others' amusement.

'You found your inner carnivore then,' Carys observed, exchanging a look with Isaac.

'Yes, well, I am eating for two, you know.'

'Isn't that an old wives' tale?' Isaac said, laughing.

'Not when I want to stuff my face, it's not.'

'You two okay to clear up?' Carys was on her feet. 'I'm going out.'

Holly looked at Isaac as they listened to Carys pounding upstairs. He said nothing, but his face said, 'See?'

'Shall we go out, too?' he said after a while. 'We could have a run out in the car, stop off for a drink somewhere.'

'Oh no, you don't have to keep me company. It's Saturday. Weren't you going out tonight?'

'Some friends are going to Brighton, to the cinema. I didn't say I'd definitely go. Don't fancy it now, to be honest.'

He leaned back in his chair, hands behind his head. Holly tried to read his expression and failed.

'Up to you. You don't have to keep me amused, though.'

She hoped she sounded as casual as she'd intended. One part of her brain fought with another: one part telling her she'd be crazy to turn down an evening with Isaac; the other wishing like merry hell that he'd take himself off to the cinema and leave her to clear her head of these stupid emotions that kept getting in the way.

'You don't want to come out with me. That's cool,' Isaac said levelly.

He stood up and ran hot water into the sink, adding a squirt of Fairy.

'Of course I do! I mean, I'd like to, but only if you wouldn't rather be doing something else.'

His hands stilled in the washing-up water. She saw his shoulders rise and fall. Taking his hands out of the sink, he shook them to waft away the suds and turned to her.

'Holly, do you have any idea how I feel about you?' He looked right into her eyes. It felt like a challenge.

'No, I don't.' Her voice was quiet, unlike her racing pulse. She was sure he must be able to hear it. 'Perhaps you'd better tell me.'

'I think I'm falling for you. In fact, I know I am.' He took a step back, averted his gaze a little. 'Sorry, I couldn't hold it in any longer.'

A beat of silence. The kitchen clock ticked loudly. She didn't know it had a tick.

'Friends, you said. You and me.' Then, in case he'd forgotten, 'When we made it up after I was horrible to you.'

'We are friends. But for me it's more.'

'It's more for me, too.'

The words were out before she could stop them.

He smiled. 'Is that true? You've got feelings for me?'

She nodded. 'But I also know I can't do anything about them. Isaac, look at me. In a couple of months, I'll be having a baby. On my own, as a single mum. Except I won't be a mum for very long.'

'So?'

'So, it's too complicated. I'm not in the right place for a relationship. There's so much going on my head, it can't deal with anything else.'

'What about your heart? Is that taken up, too? With some*body* else?'

'If you mean the father, then no. I told you, he's off the scene.'

'The trust thing, then. You told me you had trust issues.'

'I think it was you who told me.'

'Yeah.' Isaac smiled, and rubbed the top of his head. 'Sorry. It must sound as if I'm trying to find reasons why you don't want to be with me when it's quite simple. You don't, and that's that. It's okay, I get it.'

'No, Isaac, you don't. I've been fighting against the way I feel about you, and I'm losing that battle more each day. But I still don't want a relationship. It's not the right time.'

'But it could be, Holly. We could make it the right time.' He took hold of her hand, grasping it firmly. She wanted him never to let go. 'I'm in love with you. There, I've said it properly.'

Lorcan had said it, too. And look how that had turned out.

'Isaac, I don't want you to be in love with me. For a start, you've never seen me when I wasn't pregnant. You don't know me. You might look at me afterwards and see somebody totally different, and then all the feelings will go, and you'll wonder what the hell you were dreaming about. Find somebody else, somebody without all this . . . clutter.'

Isaac drew her away from the sink. 'Sit down.' She did, and so did he. 'You don't really believe that, do you? That you're a different person because you're carrying a baby?'

Holly sighed. 'No. This is what I've been telling myself all along, that I'm still me, Holly Engleby, with a mind and life of my own.'

'There you go then.'

She couldn't help smiling. He made it sound so easy. So, why wasn't it? She was in love with him, no matter how many times she told herself she wasn't. He was amazing and wonderful and caring and gorgeous, and what was more, he was in love with her, too. So he said. And she believed him. It was there, in his eyes, had been there for some time, had she been brave enough to acknowledge it.

'The washing-up water's getting cold,' she said.

* * *

They didn't go out in the end. Holly ran more hot water and washed up, leaving the crockery to drain. Isaac put the pepper and salt pots away in the cupboard. They didn't normally put them away; they lived on the kitchen table. He straightened the chairs and opened and closed the fridge, twice. Neither of them spoke.

And then, as she dried her hands, he came to her, picked up a stray strand of her hair and gently tucked it behind her ear.

'I'm not going to try and persuade you to be with me — not now, anyway. It wouldn't be fair. But there is something I want to tell you.'

They sat together on the sofa in the living room, Isaac with a glass of white wine, Holly with apple juice. She'd never wanted a glass of wine so much in her life.

'When I came back to Charnley Acre, the last thing I wanted was a relationship. Bridget and I had been together for two years. She was a radiographer at the London hospital where I worked. We'd found a flat to rent near the hospital — tiny and a bit run-down, but all we could afford. She said she didn't care, would have lived in a shoebox as long as she was with me.' He gave a little humourless laugh. 'Sounds like a cliche, doesn't it? She kept putting off moving in, though. I thought it was because it wasn't smart, and I decorated it and made as good as I could. Finally, she did move in, and we'd been there eight months when I found out she was sleeping with one of the consultants.'

'Oh no. Really?'

'Yep. It had been going for ages. Once I found out, she was brazenly honest about it.'

Isaac flinched a little, his shoulders tightening as if struck by a physical pain.

'Don't talk about it if it upsets you,' Holly said. 'You don't need to tell me any more.'

'No, I want to. I'm not playing the sympathy card here. I would just rather there not be any secrets between us.'

'Okay, so how did you find out?'

'Ha, another cliche! I came home one day and caught them in our bed. I'd taken the afternoon off and not told her.'

'Because you suspected? Is that why you went home?'

'Nope. Can't even say that. I trusted her. Why wouldn't I? I didn't leave there and then, or kick her out. We talked; I wanted to know why. She said there were affairs going on at the hospital all the time, like that made it all right. She said it was relief from the pressure of work — she worked on the diagnostic side of radiography, saw all the awful stuff first hand before the patients knew anything about it.'

'Sounds like a convenient excuse to me.' Holly wanted to hold Isaac, kiss the hurt away. But she could hardly do that. Instead, she put her glass of juice down and touched his hand briefly. 'I can't believe anyone would do that to you. I'm so sorry.'

'It's okay. I don't think about it now, except when it jumps up and bites me in the night.' He smiled. 'I gave up the lease of the flat and kipped on a mate's sofa for a while, and then the job at Cliffhaven General came up, and I thought, why not move back to Sussex?' He looked at her. 'I just wanted a bit of peace, to regroup and patch myself up and start again. And then I met you.'

Holly's turn to smile. 'The best laid plans . . . '

'Quite. I hadn't seen Bridget for a few weeks before I left London. I'd avoided the places she might be. Then she started leaving messages and texting me, saying how sorry she was, she'd made a massive mistake, and could we start again, blah blah blah. The last text I got was while I was driving down. That was why I was late, apart from taking a wrong turning. I'd stopped in a layby to read it, and text back telling her I never wanted to see or hear from her again. Except I didn't put it as politely as that.'

Holly experienced a flashback as she remembered the texts between herself and Lorcan. She recalled, too, Isaac's arrival in The Ginger Cat. Except, of course, she didn't know who he was at the time. The move from London, the new job, the thought of meeting lots of new people in a short space of time, and the recent heartache on top — his stress levels must have been through the roof. No wonder he'd seemed such a misery that first day.

'Has Bridget been in touch again since?'

'No, and I think that's the end of it. At least, I hope so.'

'Same here.' Holly bit her lower lip, glancing down at her bump.

'Oh, you mean . . . ' He saw her face. 'Okay.' He laughed. 'I think I'll change the plaque outside. Ashdown: Retreat for the Lovelorn.'

'I'm not lovelorn, and I'm certainly not retreating.'

He laughed. 'No, neither am I. Carys seems to be getting on with life, too.'

'Carys? Did she tell you about her ex-boyfriend, then?'

'She did mention it, yes.'

Holly felt her face heat up at the idea of Carys confiding in Isaac. She wondered what other secrets they'd shared.

'I am sorry, Isaac.'

'About us? Or rather, that there isn't going to be an *us*?'

She nodded.

'It's fine. Well, it's not, obviously, but perhaps one day things will change.' He raised his eyes. 'Like they do.'

'Yep, like they do.' A pause, then, 'I should move out, go back to Mum's.'

'No, please don't. Go if you want to, but not on my account.'

'I don't want to. I just thought . . . '

'You know what thought did.' He smiled.

'Okay, if you're sure.'

Holly looked at Isaac. More than a glass of wine — much more — she wanted to hold him, to be held by him. That wasn't going to happen either, was it?

★ ★ ★

'We could make it a dummy run,' Carys said, putting the cereal box back on the shelf.

'Dummy run?'

Holly yawned and rubbed at her gritty eyes. She'd had a restless night, her brain buzzing with thoughts about Isaac and then, annoyingly, Lorcan. The room had felt oppressively airless. She'd considered getting up and opening the window but decided she couldn't be bothered.

'If we're going to Cliffhaven, we can time how long it takes to get to the hospital. For when it happens.'

It was one of those rare days when neither Carys nor Holly were on duty at The Ginger Cat; Lloyd had taken on a stocky, earnest Spanish student called Alvero to tide them over the busy summer period and make up for Holly's absence. Carys was going swimming at the pool in Cliffhaven and Holly was going with her for the ride.

'No need. It takes twenty-seven minutes door-to-door, and that's with traffic.'

'Which there won't be,' Carys said. 'Babies always come in the middle of the night, just to be awkward.'

Holly laughed. 'If you say so.'

★   ★   ★

'Carys, will you be my birth partner?'

She hadn't planned the question; it just came out as they strolled along the undercliff path after devouring mega-sized Cornish pasties at the outdoor café. It might have been triggered by Carys's mention of a dummy hospital run, refuting Isaac's opinion that she was avoiding the subject. Equally, it could have been because of a subtle change in Holly's internal focus. Whatever, it was out now.

So far, she'd resisted the idea of a birth partner. Strangers — efficient professionals — helping her to deliver a child who would be handed over to strangers, had seemed right. But the image kept slipping out of place.

'You'd want your mum for that, surely?'

'I don't think she could handle it,

considering the situation.'

'Have you asked her?'

'No.'

'Well, then.'

Carys darted across the pebble-strewn walkway to stand by the flaking green balustrade. Holly followed, and stood beside her. There were few people on the beach, just a young man in jeans, his tanned torso bare, talking into a mobile phone, and two women sitting with their backs to the breakwater, faces turned upwards to the sun. Their children played on the narrow strip of sand between the pebbles and shallows, shrieking with delight every time the water reached their toes.

Carys shaded her eyes to look out to sea.

'I'd like it to be you, if you felt you could,' Holly said.

For a long moment it seemed as if Carys hadn't heard. Then she looked at Holly and gave a little shake of her head, so brief it was hardly there.

'No, I'm sorry. I'll drive you to the

hospital as I'm nearest, and I'll look after you at home afterwards, but that's as much as I can promise.'

'Okay.'

She'd meant to sound light, as if it was neither here nor there. Instead, she'd sounded peevish and put out. Which she was, if she was honest.

'Go back now, shall we?' Carys said, turning away from the sea.

As they walked back in the direction they'd come, Holly felt lost. She had no idea what to say to Carys now. It was as if by dropping the subject of the birth partner, all other subjects had been closed off, too. Carys's bouncing stride was in place, the plastic carrier bag containing her wet towel and swimsuit swinging from her hand, her head held high. Everything normal. Except it wasn't, and Holly had no idea why.

★ ★ ★

They were five minutes away from Charnley Acre when, without warning,

Carys turned off the main road, drove on a little way, then bumped the car onto an apron of cracked concrete beside a disused level crossing gate. The scent of cow parsley growing by the gate drifted in through the half open windows.

She silenced the engine but kept both hands on the steering wheel, as if she needed something to hang on to.

'You know I love you, Holls. You're my best mate and I'd do anything for you. But not that.'

'Not the birth partner thing? It's fine, I said. It won't be a picnic, even at the blunt end. It'll get messy, and I'm bound to shout at you.'

'I can do messy, and shouting if it comes to it. That's not the issue. You said your mother couldn't handle it, though we both know she could. She's the one who should be with you, Holly, not me.'

'Maybe. But I've hurt her so much already. I don't want to put her through any more if I can help it.'

Carys lifted her hands from the steering wheel and turned towards Holly. Her eyes were wide, over-bright.

'You know full well she'll be there anyway, at the first inkling you're in labour, even if it's silly o'clock and we go in my car.'

'Yes, I know she will. I don't have to nominate a birth partner. It's not compulsory. I'll just go with the flow.' And then, when Carys bit her lower lip and dropped her gaze to her lap, she added, 'Carys, it's fine. Don't think about it anymore.'

Holly meant to smile, but instead she frowned. There was something off-key about this conversation.

Carys reached for the ignition, but instead of starting the engine she pulled back.

'I'd sworn to myself I wouldn't tell you this in case it sounded as if I was using it to pressurise you into cancelling the adoption.'

Holly waited.

'I told you about Gareth, right?'

'The guy with commitment issues?'

'Yeah. I'd seen it coming, the signs that he was getting scared of how serious we were, like he wanted to backtrack. And then I fell pregnant, and scared wasn't in it. He was bloody terrified.'

'You were *pregnant*?'

This didn't sound like Carys, not the one Holly knew. The Carys Holly knew might swing through life without appearing to give a flying fig, but through it all ran an unbreakable steel cable of realism, resolve, and common sense.

'Don't sound so surprised. Anyone can make a mistake.' Carys grinned meaningfully.

She settled into the rest of her story and Holly listened without comment, though it was hard to keep quiet at times. The more she heard, the more outraged she felt on her friend's behalf. It wasn't as if youth and inexperience could be blamed for Gareth's inability to handle the situation; he was thirty-six at the time, with a couple of long-term relationships already behind him. He'd insisted Carys have a termination. If they were to have any future together, those were his terms. And Carys, her heart already torn in two, had agreed.

'I wanted that baby. That's what was so tragic about it.' She looked at Holly, the depth of her sadness showing in her eyes. 'I felt a connection with it — with him, her — but I couldn't bear to lose Gareth, so I went ahead and had it done. The craziest decision I ever made.'

Holly's mouth dried. She forced herself to speak; this wasn't about her.

'But you split up anyway?'

'Of course. Everything had changed. There was nothing left of what we'd had between us, or what I thought we'd had. At first, I thought I could get past it, that we'd have our family one day, when the right time came.' She raised her eyes. 'Like that was ever going to work.'

'It's because of me, isn't it?' Holly

said after a beat of silence, 'Me being like this has brought it all back to you. Oh God, Carys, I'm so sorry.'

'Don't be daft. It's not your fault.' Carys put her hands back on the steering wheel. Her knuckles were creamy-pale. 'But I must keep some sense of self-preservation. I have to, otherwise I'd go crazy. That's why I can't be there when your baby's born.'

'Because I'm not keeping him.'

'Yes. I wouldn't mean to get upset, but if I did and you noticed, I'd be letting you down.'

Dear Carys. Even with her heart breaking all over again, she wasn't thinking only of herself.

'I'm so sorry about what happened to you,' Holly said, 'and I'm sorry I've exposed you to all this. Sorry isn't enough, it's nothing, but it's all I've got.'

'You don't have to apologise, Holly. Your life is not my life. It's an unfortunate coincidence, that's all. But I'm fine, you don't have to worry about me. You can see why I didn't tell you before, though?'

Holly nodded. She felt teary, but she mustn't let it show. She looked out of the window at the silent railway track and abandoned signal box, sulking under a web of graffiti. No trains ran on this part of the line now; hadn't done since some politician back in history closed it down. Dad used to say what a tragedy it was.

'There will be other chances for both of us to have babies, in the future,' Holly said.

'How can we be sure, Holly? Nothing's certain in this life. Nothing.'

★　★　★

It was around half past ten. Holly had just gone to bed when she heard a tap on the door and Carys put her head round.

'Can I come in?'

'Of course.'

Carys was wearing a grey velour

bathrobe, frayed around the sleeve edges and loosely tied so that it fell open, revealing the pale half-moons of her breasts. Her face was pink, the ends of her hair damp from her bath. She sat on the end of the bed.

'I'll do it. I'll be your birth partner. Put me down with the midwife, or whatever it is you do. When the time's getting close, I'll make sure I'm no further away than The Ginger Cat.' She held up a hand. 'And before you ask me if I'm sure, I've thought about it and I want to do it. I want to be there for you, so don't try and stop me.'

Holly felt the grin spreading across her face.

'I wasn't going to.' There'd be no point, she could see that by the set of Carys's chin. 'Thanks, Carys. Thank you.'

'On one condition.'

'What's that?'

'That you ask your mother, make out she's the first one you asked, and if she says yes then I'll step down.'

Holly thought for a moment, tried to visualise how it would be in the delivery room, what would actually happen . . . apart from her being in labour, of course. She realised she had very little idea. She'd been to the classes at the medical centre, sat through the talks and films. But apart from one or two nuggets of information that had slipped through, like the stages of labour and the types of pain relief on offer — and even those were hazy — she'd shut herself off and let it all slide by unnoticed, willing the session to be over so she could be released, back into the real world.

'I've got a condition, too. If at any time it gets too much, then you must leave, and I'll know. I'll understand.'

'Okay. But ask your mum.'

'I will.'

Holly crossed her fingers beneath the duvet. It was Carys she wanted. Mum might be there, too — almost certainly she would — but with her friend there the dynamic would be different, less intense, more manageable. Despite her doubts, Carys would hold it together, she felt certain.

Carys had one foot up on the bed, her chin resting on her knee as she picked at a stray flake of electric-blue nail polish. She'd shared her secret with Holly — nobody else knew apart from one friend in Wales, and the ex-boyfriend himself. It must have cost her something to do that. It was time for Holly to give something of herself in return.

13

At some point during the telling of Holly's story, Carys had moved so that they were alongside each other. Carys was lying, face up, on top of the duvet, her head on the second pillow, the fingers of one hand laced with Holly's.

'Did you tell anyone what happened? Somebody at uni? A doctor?'

'No, it would have been like opening the proverbial can of worms. The questions, the looks of doubt, as if I was making the whole thing up. I couldn't face it. I didn't even tell Bethany.'

'Or your mother?'

'God, no! Imagine that?'

'Yeah, imagine.'

'Anyway, it was partly my fault. He knew I still had those feelings for him, after I'd fallen into bed with him the day before. I was stupid and naïve, thinking he'd leave it at that.'

'No, Holly!' Carys's head was off the pillow, her eyes blazing. 'The way he treated you was *never* your fault. *Nothing* excuses that sort of behaviour. You do know that, don't you?'

'Yes. Normally, yes.'

'Normally, my backside.' Carys gave a snort of derision.

She was right to be angry. Holly would have been, too, in her position. But looking at it from a different perspective, from the inside instead of out, it wasn't that simple.

★   ★   ★

The day when Lorcan had turned up at the house with the Chelsea buns, he hadn't forced himself on her, not in any shape or form. She'd let those kisses happen because she'd wanted them, and had sex with him willingly. More than willingly — the little demon she carried around with her, the one that tapped her on the shoulder and urged her to have some fun and live dangerously once in a while, had seen to that. At least she'd had the presence of mind to fix herself up with the morning-after pill. She'd nipped out to the pharmacy around four o'clock as it was starting to get dark. The warning from the pharmacist that there was a small chance of failure had barely sunk in. She'd be fine. But she mustn't let it happen again.

Bethany and Ruomi had texted to say they were heading back to Birmingham at the weekend, ready for the start of term on Monday. The rest of the house would be full by then, too. But on Friday evening, Holly was there alone, her other house-sharers having gone out. She could have gone out, too — Erin had got over the worst of her cold and was meeting Amber at the pub — but she still had work to do. If she put the hours in, she would have the weekend free to spend time with Bethany and the others.

The doorbell sounded at around eight-thirty.

'Hello, you,' Lorcan said as she opened the door. 'I brought wine.'

'Sorry, I can't. I'm working. Nice of you to think of me, though.' Brisk, but not unfriendly.

'Aw, come on, Holly. It's your favourite, look.'

He held up the bottle. She didn't even have a favourite wine.

She stayed firm and didn't open the door to let him in. It wasn't that she was afraid of what might happen. She'd promised herself she wouldn't get involved again, and this time she meant it.

'Yesterday was a mistake. We're over, Lorcan, and we shouldn't have got carried away, but we have to put it behind us. I'll see you around, okay?'

'Okay.' He'd nodded, turned on the step as if he was leaving, then spun back round. 'Holly, I can't stop thinking about you. We were good when were together, you know that. Why throw what we had away for the sake of a few essays?'

Holly sighed. Without meaning to, she'd leaned against the door, making a bigger gap. Lorcan was now inside the hallway.

'We've been through all this before and I'm not going to repeat it. I thought you understood. You need to leave me alone now.'

She tempered this with a half-smile. Lorcan dipped his gaze for a second. When he looked up again, he was smiling, but his eyes were sad. She knew that look. It made her heart squeeze.

She had nobody to blame but herself. It should have been a clean break when she finished with him back in the summer; she should have made it clearer, been surer of her own intentions and stuck to them. She'd thought they were of the same mind, that they could be friends, but after yesterday it was clear that was never going to work. She said as much to Lorcan. He seemed to accept it, but she was on her guard now. They'd been here before.

'Lorcan, I'm sorry about yesterday. It was lovely, of course, but we shouldn't have. It's complicated things. But what's done is done. We just have to forget it now and move on.'

'Yeah, you're right. You're too damn sexy, that's your problem.' He laughed, rolling his eyes.

'Well, I shall try not to be in future.'

'Me, too. I'll order my hairline to recede and grow a beer paunch.' He patted his flat stomach.

Better. Joshing, sending themselves up. Fine. But Lorcan didn't leave.

'It's cold out there. Brass monkey weather.'

'Well, I suppose you'd better come in now you're here,' Holly said, forgetting he was already in. 'Just for a quick warm-up, though. Forget the wine. I was going to make hot chocolate, if that's of any interest?'

'That would be great, if it's not too much trouble. I'll get going after that. I should be working, too. I *do* understand, Holly. I get how it has to be between us from now on, and I promise to behave.' He stood the bottle of wine down beside the skirting and gave a comical salute. 'Scout's Honour.'

★   ★   ★

'I can't believe you let him in,' Carys said. 'Not after what the pair of you had got up to the day before.'

'I know, and neither could I afterwards. Even at the time, I knew it was a bad idea. But he looked so crestfallen standing there, and he looked frozen, like he'd been walking around the streets for ages.'

'You're too soft for your own good, you know that?'

'Probably am.' Holly cradled her bump covered by the duvet. 'I'm also an idiot.'

'This time I won't disagree. So go on, what happened next?'

'I felt totally in control. I put the gas fire on in the communal living room and told him to sit there while I made the drinks. Then, after we'd drunk them and I stood up to take the mugs back to the kitchen, he gave me that look again, the puppy-dog look. And before I knew where I was, he was leaning in for a kiss. I ducked it. I got cross, told him he was taking advantage, and he'd better leave now. I wasn't afraid or anything, just bloody furious — with him for trying it on again, with myself for sleeping with him the day before. And for believing he'd accepted the situation.' She turned to look at Carys. 'Yes, I know. *I know.* I hate myself for being so stupid!'

'Okay, don't get upset. Just tell me what happened, in your own time.'

'Somehow he got me by the wall. I must have put the chocolate mugs down, or he took them from me, I don't remember, but he held my hands by my sides and started kissing me. He was persistent but not forceful or rough, not then, but my back was against the wall and I felt all the power go out of me, like someone had pulled the plug. I moved my head away and told him to stop. He didn't. He kissed me again . . . or he tried to. I think he missed that time. And then I pushed him, not hard, just enough to get him off me. He held my hands tighter, away at the sides, and he pushed against me. I stamped on his foot, I remember that, but I only had socks on.'

'God, Holly, are you telling me he *raped* you?'

'No, no. Not that. I don't think he would have gone that far, I honestly don't.'

★ ★ ★

'Don't push me away. Please, Holly, you know how I feel about you.' Lorcan was still gripping her hands, but he'd stopped trying to kiss her, and there was a little distance between them now. 'It's because of him, isn't it? The bloke I saw you at the party with before Christmas, the one who lives here. Stephen.'

'Stefan. And no, it's nothing to do with him. I'm not seeing him, I'm not seeing anyone.' Why she'd bothered to put him straight on that, she had no idea. It was none of his business.

'Yeah, right.'

His tone was disbelieving, but he let go of her hands. There were tears in his eyes. She slid slowly to one side, away from him.

'Lorcan, I'd like you to go. Please? I can see you're upset and I'm so sorry I hurt you, but you have to leave now.'

His face changed, hardened. He looked like someone she didn't know. He grabbed her by the wrist, encircling it tightly. He wore a ring on his little finger. It dug into her skin.

'You're hurting me! Let go!'

'Sorry, sorry.'

He let her go, but his hand found her chin, cupping it gently but firmly. She thought he was going to try and kiss her, but as she moved to free herself, his grip tightened, and he shoved her head backwards so that it hit the wall with a dull thud.

He took two steps back, eyes wide, appalled at what he'd done. Holly stared back at him, frozen with shock.

⋆ ⋆ ⋆

'Then he left. He almost ran out of the room, up the stairs, and all the time he kept saying 'I'm sorry, I'm sorry' over and over, and I heard the front door bang shut. I had a lump on the back of my head for two days, and I've still got a mark where his ring jabbed in.'

She raised her hand and pointed at the miniscule white line on the outside of her wrist, although with only the bedside light on, it was practically invisible.

'And all the time, you were expecting his child. The morning-after pill didn't work. You were pregnant.'

'Yes.'

'I take it Lorcan has no idea?'

'There's a very slim chance he found out through the grapevine, but it isn't likely, otherwise I'd have heard from him by now.' She'd stopped worrying about Bethany's revelation. Whatever the situation, there was nothing she could do about it.

'What a bastard.' Carys blew out air.

'I don't think of him like that. He's not a wicked person. I went out with him for long enough. I should know.'

'Oh Holly, you can't keep making excuses for him!'

'I'm not. I'm just stating the facts as I see them, that's all.'

Holly sensed the tension in Carys as she lay beside her, and expected a torrent of anger and grief. Instead, she rolled over onto her side, flung her arm around Holly and held her. She could feel Carys's breath against her cheek.

They stayed like that for what seemed like a very long time. Eventually, Carys sat up, shook her hair so that the bob fell neatly into place, and retied the belt of her dressing gown.

'Can I get you a drink or anything?'

She sounded normal, ordinary. Holly

blessed her for that. She sat up.

'No, I'm good, thanks. Carys, if I were to keep this child, and one day he asks who his father is, I don't think I could lie outright and tell him I don't know. And if I told him the truth, that his father was unpredictable and . . . obsessive — that's what he is — and that's why I couldn't have him in our lives, how's he supposed to deal with that?'

'Kids are pretty resilient. If he was adopted, he'd have to know about that at some point, and deal with it. Perhaps if you explained about his biological father when he's older and able to understand, then . . . '

'No. It's better this way.' She looked at Carys. 'Maybe you think it's fairer if I come clean and let Lorcan know. But then I'd be linked to him forevermore, and I'd always remember I'd fallen out of love with him, and what he did to me, and that the baby didn't come from a loving relationship.'

Carys began to speak but Holly hushed her.

'And supposing he turned on our child one day, like he turned on me? Think how horrendous that would be.'

'I *know*, honey. I'm agreeing with you. He needs to be out of your life, both your lives. But you might come to regret the adoption, and that's something that *would* stay with you all your life. Oh, I know I'm being hard saying that, but somebody has to.'

Holly pulled a face. 'Somebody already has. My mum.'

'She talks a lot of sense, your mum.'

Carys grinned, lightening the moment. But there was something behind it, something in the slight drawing together of her eyebrows that spoke of deeper secrets. And Holly knew she was thinking of her own baby, the baby that never was, and how she lived with that regret.

She held out her hand. Carys gave her a quizzical look and took it. Holly gave Carys's hand a gentle squeeze, meeting her friend's gaze, willing across the message that she understood. Carys waited a second, then gave a little nod. 'I'm okay,' it said. 'Or if I'm not, I will be.'

Their smiles collided.

14

August. Most days, at least two coaches at a time stood in the council car park at the end of the village. They didn't stop for very long — Charnley Acre might be a typical picturesque Sussex village, but it didn't take hours to see it all — and then their load of trippers would be transported on to the next delight on the schedule. But not before they'd sampled the homely fare in the village's prettiest café, The Ginger Cat.

'When's your due date, my lovely?'

Jo looked Holly dubiously up and down as she came through to the back carrying a loaded tray from her latest round of table-clearing.

'October the fourth.'

'That's less than two months away! Hasn't it passed quickly?'

No, Holly thought. *It feels like I've been like this since the beginning of time*. But she just smiled. She knew what was coming next.

'Well, whenever you want to finish, just tell us. Your health comes first. There'll still be a job for you here afterwards, if you want one. You'll be able to sort out your childcare, I'm sure. The other young mums in the village seem to manage.'

Unsurprisingly, Jo was interested in Holly's plans; she needed to know where she stood, staff-wise. Of course, she had no idea that childcare wouldn't be an issue. But now wasn't the time for another of those difficult conversations.

'Thanks, Jo. My plans are a bit woolly at the moment, though. Sorry, that's not a lot of help, is it?'

Jo took the tray from Holly. 'Ah, no worries, love. You'll want a decent bit of time to be with the baby before you think about work again, and Alvero says he'll be here for as long as we need him. He's extending his stay with his host family, lucky for us. Plus, we've got

Carys, until she gets a better offer.'

Jo had deliberately raised her voice, drawing a quizzical look from Carys, who was stencilling cat shapes into the foam on the tops of three cappuccinos.

'What've I done now?'

'Nothing I've found out about,' Jo said, laughing. 'I was saying we've still got you when Holly has to give it up.'

'Which could be any day now,' Carys said. 'She looks fit to drop, and I don't mean sleep-wise.'

'That reminds me,' Lloyd called from the kitchen. 'I must put that notice in the window about Bertha's kittens. They'll be ready for homing soon. Had no idea she was expecting when we took her in, did we, Jo?'

A couple at the nearest table looked at each other and smirked.

'Charming.' Holly sniffed before the grin broke free. 'I'd like to carry on with the hours I'm doing now till the end of this month, it that's all right with you and Lloyd, Jo? After that, I doubt I'll be able to get through the door, let alone squeeze behind this counter.'

'This is true,' Carys said.

Holly rolled her eyes and went to take more orders.

Mum would be pleased at her decision to stop work at the end of the month. She'd been on at her to stop for a while now, all in Holly's best interests, of course. But the tips were good at this time of year; and added to the wages, it meant she had a decent amount coming in. Mum wouldn't see her short, but the thought of being dependent on her to top up the benefits she'd receive didn't feel right. Not at her age, and never mind the circumstances.

As for her plans for after the birth, woolly was an apt way to describe them. Baby-brain, that was what it was. She'd imagined that came after the birth, but hers had kicked in early, blurring the outlines of her ambitions until she was no longer sure they were there at all. *Poor excuse. Not good enough, Holly.* She must make the effort to get in touch with her course leader and discuss her return to Birmingham. She wouldn't make the start of year, but January might be an option. Or she may be required to start her second year again from scratch, in which case she'd have to wait around until the following September, and get a job in the meantime. Somewhere more mentally challenging and financially rewarding than The Ginger Cat.

Holly pushed away the idea that university had lost its appeal. She needed a plan and now she had one. It would do, for now.

★ ★ ★

Laura and Clayton went on holiday to the Lake District. They were renting a whitewashed cottage with a slate roof near Ambleside, and had invited Holly along. It was tempting, but the long car journey didn't appeal, nor would it have been fair to ask for more time off from the café when she was about to leave altogether.

She spent some time at Spindlewood while her mother was away. As well as checking on the house, it was time she could spend alone with her thoughts. On sunny afternoons, she would wander through the rooms, picking up things randomly, gazing at pictures which had been on the same walls for years, reminding herself of the unique way the light slanted into the various rooms, the patches of shadow where the sun never reached, the door that never quite closed properly, and the scent of beeswax in the panelled dining room.

These solitary journeys through the house always culminated in the circular book-lined turret room; her mother's thinking place. When Holly was small, the turret room had made a great den — a magical hideaway where she and her friends would invent games with ridiculous rules and form secret societies demanding the memorising of a string of ever-changing passwords.

Holly stood by the window in the

turret room and sent wishes to the sky for her child to have a den as special as hers, a childhood as warm and safe.

⋆　⋆　⋆

When Mum came home, Holly sensed a change in her. She smiled a lot more than usual, in a private kind of way. Eventually, prompted by Holly's none-too-subtle questioning while they were driving back to Ashdown after supper at Spindlewood, she confessed that she and Clayton had finally talked properly about living together.

'Don't go getting all excited,' Mum said as Holly thumped the dashboard in a moment of triumph. 'I know you think we should, but it's not done and dusted yet. We have to be completely sure.'

'What happened to spontaneity, Mother?' Holly glanced down at her bulging dress. 'Actually, don't answer that.'

It was a move in the right direction,

though; Mum and Clayton were a perfect match. He would make her happy, Holly was sure of it.

For a moment, she felt as if she were the mother and Laura the child. The baby kicked lightly; more of a tickle, really, reminding her of who was who in this set-up. Holly giggled.

'All right?' Mum glanced at her, smiling.

'Fine.'

⋆ ⋆ ⋆

August drifted on. The days were either blue-skied and golden or sultry and overcast, and relentlessly dry. Around Charnley Acre, the rain-deprived fields were baked hard, the crops ripened to the colour of bread crust.

Clayton rang to remind them to water the garden at Ashdown. 'Not just the odd sprinkle when you feel like it. Give it a regular dousing.' The old metal watering can with its spray top missing, which Carys found behind a bush in the garden, was clearly more trouble than it was worth, and the others wouldn't let Holly lift it while full. So they clubbed together and bought a hosepipe with an adjustable head. Holly watched Carys and Isaac sparring in the back garden with this bit of kit, spraying each other 'accidentally', and felt a little left out. It was because of Isaac, of course. If he still had feelings for her, he was hiding them well. Which was all to the good, of course, and yet she couldn't let go of the idea that here was a love that was going to waste.

He was going out more than he used to, in the evenings and at weekends. Holly watched surreptitiously from the window as he sped off in the car, and experienced a dip in spirits before she pulled herself together. She'd wanted it this way. He was doing as she'd asked and getting on with his life, just as she would hers when it was all over and everything was back to normal.

The three of them still spent evenings

at The Goose and Feather, especially if any decent bands were playing. Then the pub would be full, and the chances were that they'd separate as they caught sight of various friends. Saul Fielding was home from agricultural college in Suffolk; Holly hadn't seen him for ages. She forgot she was hugely pregnant until she went to hug him and Saul performed a double-take, and they both burst into laughter. He showed her a photo on his phone of a healthy-looking girl with a mop of dark curly hair. She was taking Equestrian Studies. Holly kissed him on the cheek and wished him well.

On her last day at The Ginger Cat, the Friday before August Bank Holiday, Jo and Lloyd presented her with a Moses basket lined with red gingham fabric. Tucked beside the pillow was an envelope. It contained one hundred pounds.

'From us, and some of the regulars chipped in as well,' Jo said. 'It'll help towards things for the baby.'

Holly couldn't speak. She'd never told them. It hadn't been a deliberate omission; the right time had never come. They were always so busy. Anyway, how could she have just come out with something like that?

She found her voice eventually, thanked Jo and Lloyd, said she would drop a thank-you card in, and left carrying the basket. She'd never felt like such a fraud.

★　★　★

Two weeks later, on Sunday morning, her grandmother rang.

'I've been thinking, Holly, and I wondered if you'd like to come and stay with me for a few days — a week, as long as you like — when it's all over. It might help to . . . well, it would be somewhere *different*.'

There it was; no judgemental words, no undertone in her voice. Just love and support.

'Oh, Gran . . . '

Isaac looked up from the paper he'd been reading. He must have heard the catch in her voice. *Okay?* he mouthed.

Holly nodded and mouthed back, *My gran.* Isaac gave her a smile loaded with feeling and meaning, and went back to his paper.

'What do you say, Holly?' Gran sounded so cheery and bright. Holly wished she was right here in the room; she'd have liked to kiss her.

'It sounds lovely. Thanks, Gran.'

She hadn't thought about that part of it, immediately afterwards, when the baby had gone. Her mind had swished over it and rushed on to the future, however hazy. Being with Gran in her pretty house on the edge of the New Forest could be just what she'd need. It was impossible to tell right now, though. She said as much to her grandmother.

'That's all right, darling. You just let me know when the time comes, and if you fancy it, I'll come straight over and drive you back. We'll have some proper girl time, just you and me. Pamper ourselves. Your mum will be back at her school by then. She'll like to know you're in safe hands.'

I don't deserve this, Holly thought. She pasted on a smile, as if her grandmother could see. 'Yes, I'll be in touch. Love you, Gran.'

'Love you, too, darling.'

Holly went up to her room. She felt like crying. She *always* felt like crying these days, as if there was a balloon full of tears behind her eyes waiting to burst. If she was about to give in to it now, she didn't want Isaac to see. She'd already given him too much to cope with. She must stay strong and not implode into an emotional mess at the slightest thing.

She opened the window and leaned on the sill, breathing deeply until the tearfulness subsided and she felt normal again. After a while, she heard the front door open; Carys, back from her run. Holly used the bathroom then went downstairs. Carys lay in a heap on the sofa, her feet in grubby trainers hanging off the end.

'Get us some water, Holls.'

'I don't know why you torture yourself.' Holly laughed, and fetched a glass of water from the kitchen.

'You're coming running with me, after. We have to get you fit again, back into shape. Although, knowing your luck, you'll ping back to a size ten in no time.'

'Don't hold your breath, on either count. Where's Isaac?'

The paper he'd been reading was on the chair he'd vacated. Carys sat up and took a long drink of water, then thumbed towards the front door. 'He went out as I came in.'

'Oh,' Holly said.

He hadn't said he was going out. Not that he needed to.

Carys looked up at Holly. 'He's in love with you.'

'I know.'

'And?'

'And nothing.'

* ⋆ ⋆

The baby was restless, as restless as his cramped conditions allowed him to be. He'd picked up on her own mood, Holly surmised, as she wiped the kitchen floor on hands and knees on Monday morning, after Carys and Isaac had left for work. The physical challenge made the result all the more satisfying. She cleaned out the food cupboards next, standing on the step-stool — which the others wouldn't have allowed, had they been there — while she turfed out jars of congealed honey and pots of dried herbs way past their sell-by dates. She knew what her mother would say if she could see her. Nesting instinct. A sign of imminent birthing. *Nope, wrong, Mother. It's only September.*

She was bored with cleaning now, anyway. Before her assault on the kitchen, she'd run the vacuum around, downstairs and up, and done some ironing, most of which consisted of

Isaac's work shirts. He did his own washing and ironing, of course, but it wouldn't hurt to do him a favour; he'd done plenty for her. It wasn't as if she didn't have the time.

Five minutes later, having put on a long grey cardigan over her yellow print dress and slung on her shoulder bag, Holly left the house.

The days had a fresher feel now. They'd even had rain, occasional showers that came mostly before dawn, greening the lawns and sweetening the flowers. Her steps were light — as light as they could be — as she set off along Parsley Street with no particular desti-nation in mind. Turning into the high street, she stopped at the newsagents for a tube of soft mints. Glancing across the road at The Ginger Cat, she wondered whether to call in for a cup of tea and a chat, but she wouldn't be able to resist a slice of cake to go with it. Definitely not a good idea; she'd wolfed down three of Carys's brownies while she'd watched telly last night. There'd be a lot more than baby-weight to lose at this rate. She unwrapped the mints and put one in her mouth as she walked on.

Once she'd passed the high street and the row of cottages beyond, and reached the crossroads, she didn't have to think about where she was going: up Charnley Hill, then down the public footpath beside the woods. She glanced towards the gates of Spindlewood as she passed. Clayton's green van was parked at the top of the drive — she could just see the end of it, the rear doors open. He'd be working on the garden, no doubt. A garden of that size needed endless upkeep.

She couldn't see her mother's car, but she wouldn't expect to. Term had begun, and Laura was back at the chalkface. Holly smiled as she thought of all the kids, special ones at that, who had been taught and nurtured by her mother over the years. Complain she might, but the truth was that Mum loved her job. Holly hoped she'd find something she could do with equal passion. Which she would, in time.

But she didn't want to think about the future today; there'd been enough of that lately. She wandered slowly on up the hill, then stopped at the top by the signpost. The faint breeze at the highest point held a hint of autumn. Holly stood and enjoyed the soft feel of it on her face. The harvest was in, the fields stubbly brown. In the distance, a red tractor rode the undulations of the empty landscape. From here, it looked like a toy.

A tightening sensation, deep down, took her by surprise. Her hand found its way automatically to the lower part of her bulge, seeking out the source of the feeling. A moment later, she felt it again, like a hand clutching her from inside. Uncomfortable, alien, but not painful. Were these the Braxton Hicks things she'd been told about? Other women at the clinic said they'd been having those, but she never had. Until now. Perhaps she'd overdone it with the floor cleaning. She waited, hand on bump, to see if it would happen again. It didn't. She went through the gate and set off down the footpath, treading carefully in her trainers to avoid the ruts in the path on the steep descent.

The woods on her left were quiet and still, and aromatic with damp moss and wild garlic. To her right, a thrush perched on the fence, tilted its head, then flew off as she approached. She'd loved coming here when she was a child. Parts of the woods were fenced off but there was still a way in — several, in fact, known only to the locals. If you managed to get right to the heart of the woods, there was a tiny pond obscured by undergrowth, covered in green scum, but magical in its secrecy. You couldn't get a baby buggy down here, not easily. It would have to be one of those sling things. Then a shoulder ride when he was bigger, until he could slip-slide down the path on his own.

Holly gave her head a little shake to

check her thoughts. Seconds later, they were back. This time she visualised another familiar playground; the pebbly curve of Cliffhaven beach, bounded by rocks big enough to climb on. Only when the tide was out was there ever enough sand to build a castle.

She would teach him about the tides. Or somebody would.

Except it was impossible to imagine that person being anyone but herself.

The unseen hand gripped again, and this time Holly drew in a breath. Well, if that was a Braxton Hicks, they could keep them. She'd wait for the real thing, thank you very much.

The curve in the footpath was in sight. Just beyond that, it was only a minute or so back to the crossroads. She would have a lie down when she got home. Her body was telling her there'd been enough activity for one day.

Nearing the bottom of the footpath, Holly came to the metal gate opening onto the field where she'd sat with

Bethany. Perhaps a rest would be a good idea. It was so peaceful here. The pretend contractions had gone; there was no hurry to get home. She had one hand on the latch when a wall of pain rose up, making her gasp.

Please, no. It couldn't be happening for real, could it? Not now, not here, without a single soul in sight. She took a long, deep breath. Her bulge beneath her pressed hand felt unusually rigid.

Oh God.

No, no, she must keep calm. There was no reason to panic. Even if this was the real thing — unlikely, but *if* it was — as long she kept her head it would all be fine. Unzipping her shoulder bag, she reached inside for her mobile and found only her purse, keys, and the packet of mints. She could see her phone now, on the hall shelf at home.

Right then. Keep walking. Get to the crossroads, and back to the village. Easy. But the next steps she took made her legs feel shaky. Holly looked about. Nobody. The red tractor was nearer than before. It was trundling along by the hedgerow at the bottom of the field. She stood on the bottom rung of the gate, extended her arm and waved madly. She thought the person in the tractor cab waved back, but she couldn't be sure. She unlatched the gate and went through, walked a little way on across the tufty grass, then waved both arms. At the same time, she called out: 'Hey, over here!'

The tractor carried on along its original route. Of course, he hadn't heard her over the noise of the engine. She windmilled her arms again and the vehicle began turning in a wide circle, moving closer. She could see its driver now, his eyes on her.

She stumbled forward, forgetting about the uneven surface, righting herself as the tractor grew near, painfully slowly, until it stopped just yards away. The driver jumped down from the cab.

'Was it me you was after?'

He looked around sixty, squarely built, with solid shoulders, a thatch of silver-grey hair, and old-fashioned bushy side whiskers framing a sun-browned creased face. He wore balding cord trousers, a checked shirt with the sleeves rolled up, and wellingtons.

Holly began to answer but another spasm whisked her voice away.

'What've we got 'ere then?' the tractor driver said, scrutinising Holly. 'Got caught on the hop, have we?'

Ten out of ten. 'I've had a couple of pains, nothing much. I'm not due for three weeks so it can't be happening yet, but I've forgotten my phone and I need to get home, if you could help?'

The next pain was shorter, sharper, doubling her over.

The man shook his head. 'It's happening, all right. I should know. The missus had five of 'em.' He gave a gruff laugh. Holly couldn't see what there was to laugh about.

'If you could just ring an ambulance for me, I could meet it up there, on the road.'

'Nope. I haven't got one of those

mobile things. The missus is always telling me to get one.' The folds in his face opened out into a fatherly smile. 'Not much use you knowing that now. You'd better come with me.'

Holly found herself ushered round to the other side of the cab. His strong arms hoisted her easily onto the seat.

'You're lucky. I only had a passenger seat fitted last week to give the grandkids a ride, otherwise you'd have been on the floor.'

The tractor lurched forwards. Holly lurched with it.

'I live in the village, one of the back streets.'

'And that's always supposing I could get us down there. No, your best bet's the ambulance, like you said. I'll get us onto the top road and then we'll see what we can do.'

See what we can do? Was that all?

'Aw . . . ' The pain struck again. Holly clutched the edges of her seat.

'Now, then. You'll be all right with me.'

How could he be so calm? And couldn't this ruddy tractor go any faster?

She had a thought. 'Can you take me to Spindlewood? It's a house halfway down Charnley Hill.' Mum wouldn't be home yet, but perhaps Clayton would still be there.

'I knows it. Lovely old place. Who lives there, then?'

'I do. No, my mother does.'

The driver smiled and patted Holly's hand. 'Spindlewood it is then. I can manage that.'

He braked, got out and opened the top gate. A minute later, the tractor lumbered onto the road.

'First little 'un, is it?'

'Yes.' Holly gritted her teeth as another pain flooded through her. 'First babies are always late, they say.'

'Whoever told you that was makin' it up.'

'Clearly.' Holly grimaced.

It could still be a false alarm, though. Any moment now, the pains would go away. Even so, that was the last time she'd go walking on her own.

It seemed to take forever for the tractor to turn into Spindlewood's entrance and negotiate the upward sloping drive. There was obviously nobody at home. Clayton's van had gone. Her mother had not, by some miracle, come home early. Holly had the key, though; she kept it on the ring with her own.

'If you could just see me inside, er . . . '

'Neville.'

'. . . I'll be fine. My mother will be home soon.'

The next wave of pain had her clutching at the door frame for support.

Neville raised a bushy eyebrow and took the key from Holly's hand. 'I don't think we wanna be hanging about for 'er.'

Once they were in, Neville picked up the landline phone from the hall. 'Now, you go and sit down, and I'll sort you out.' A broad fingertip was already punching out 999.

'Oh, really, I don't think . . . aaar-rggh!'

'There, there, all done.' He gave Holly an appraising look. 'Mebbe a bedroom would be best. Think you can get upstairs?'

'I think so. Come up with me?'

Stranger or not, she did not want to be left alone now, not for one minute.

Neville waggled his feet out of his wellingtons and kicked them aside. 'I'm right behind you.'

★　★　★

Holly writhed on top of the bed in her old bedroom. Neville leaned in the doorway, arms folded, as if he was keeping guard.

'Did they say how long they'd be?'

'Couldn't tell. I told them it was an emergency, like.'

Holly rolled onto her side, pulling her knees up as another contraction rolled in.

'The missus had all hers at home,' Neville said conversationally.

'I'm not *at* home. I'm not ready, I haven't got all my stuff, and my birth partner's down in the village. I can't have the baby now . . . Oww!'

'Looks like you haven't got a choice, lovey.' Neville came right into the room and crossed to the window. 'Here we go. Action stations!' He was off down the stairs.

Moments later, he was back, accompanied by a tall thirty-something guy with copper-coloured hair, wearing black trousers and a blue polo shirt with a logo on it. He was carrying a large black case.

'Hal. First Responder.' He flashed a badge and a smile.

'*Thank* you,' Holly said, more to the heavens than to this Hal person.

She'd be safely on her way to hospital in a minute. She sat up, swung her legs down off the bed, and craned to look out of the window. 'Where's the ambulance?' The only vehicles on the

340

forecourt were the tractor and a Mini Cooper.

'Ah, no. Only me for now. I'll radio for a midwife in a sec.'

'Only you?' Holly wailed. 'What the . . . oh!' The pain whizzed through her. She fought it, arching her back and leaning backwards on the bed. 'I can't, I can't do it on my own . . . '

'Back on the bed . . . What's your name?'

'Holly. Holly Engleby.'

'Well, you just lie back there, Holly Engleby, try to relax, and we'll have a little look-see.'

Neville moved swiftly away from the doorway. She heard him going downstairs. Now it was just her and another complete stranger called Hal. No Mum, no Carys, no midwife. What the hell. She was way past caring.

*   *   *

A layer of crackly polythene beneath her. A towel. A bowl. Implements, shiny bright. Entonox, two gasps, no time for more. Sunlight on the ceiling. A roomful of silence. Apart from the animal-like howls that seemed not to come from her but from the bottom of a cave.

★ ★ ★

'Congratulations,' Hal said. 'You have a daughter.'

A girl!

Of course, Holly thought.

Of course.

15

Mum came home half an hour after the midwife had arrived from Cliffhaven to take over from Hal. Holly was sitting up, the baby cradled in her arms, a mug of tea and a sandwich on the bedside table.

'Whose is the tractor?' Holly heard. Neville must still be here. Then, 'Holly? *Holly!*'

Footsteps up the stairs, hurrying. Mum burst into the room, to be met by Holly's beaming smile.

'Oh. Oh, Holly,' Laura said. 'Are you all right, darling? I guessed when I saw the car with the badge outside. What a *shock!*'

'I'm fine, Mum.'

'Oh, Holly, just *look* at him.'

Holly glanced down at the tiny face peeping from the blue-and-white fringed blanket — the softest that Penny, the midwife, could find in the chest on the landing.

'Her.' Holly smiled. 'It's a girl, Mum, and she's perfect.'

'Oh!' Mum said again, and burst into tears.

'I'll give you some time together,' Penny said, and slipped from the room.

She knows, Holly thought. She has my notes.

Mum's tears vanished as quickly as they'd begun as she concentrated on the facts and practicalities. Holly told her story and gave her mother the answers she needed. The baby was a little small but healthy, Holly herself was fine, and no, they didn't need to go to hospital.

She could sense Mum's internal fight, see the maelstrom of emotion through the expression in her eyes. But wait. She had to get this right. This was forever.

There was a tap on the door and Penny was back.

'I don't how you feel about this, but

the farmer chappie wondered if he could see the baby before he went? What'll I tell him?'

'Yes, let him come up,' Holly said. 'I need to thank him for rescuing me.'

Neville stood at the end of the bed and peered long and hard at the baby before his creased face broke into a grin. 'Well now, you've got a little cracker there.' He nodded slowly. 'A little cracker.'

'I know. Come round here, Neville.'

He hesitated, then moved round the bed, closer to Holly. Stretching above the baby, she planted a kiss on Neville's cheek. 'Thank you. You were marvellous. I don't know what I would have done without you.'

He smiled, rubbing the place where the kiss had landed. 'Get on with you. Nothing new to me, all this. The missus had five, all of 'em born at home.'

'Yes, you said.'

With a last look at the baby, and a nod towards Laura and Penny, Neville padded out of the room.

'He's got a hole in his sock,' Mum observed. 'A great big one on his heel.'

'His missus will see to that,' Penny said, and they all laughed.

★ ★ ★

Carys arrived; Holly heard her unmistakeable tread on the stairs before she reached her room. Mum must have called her when she'd gone to turn the heating up again — the room was already baking — make more tea, and sort out food for later. Penny had just left and would be back in the morning.

'I can't *believe* I missed it after all that!' Carys plonked herself down on the bed and gathered Holly into a hug. 'You did it all by yourself!'

'Not quite by myself. I had Hal. He was pretty marvellous. Not that I noticed at the time.'

'I know but . . . oh, Holly.' Carys's eyes were on the baby now. 'She's *beautiful* . . . ' Her voice broke on the word. Like Laura, she turned to practical things. 'I brought your bag, the one you packed for hospital, and the clothes and nappies and stuff from the chest on the landing.'

Holly's holdall and several carrier bags were on the floor, by the bed. 'Great,' she said. 'The midwife brought an outfit and some basic things for her, but that's all she's got.'

'I brought the Moses basket, too, and some clothes and stuff for you. It's all down in the car. I'll go and fetch it, then you can tell me what else you need.' She bounced up from the bed, fished in her pocket of her jeans, and brought out Holly's mobile phone. 'And *this*.' She threw it onto the bed. '*Honestly*, Holly!'

'Yep, I'm an idiot. We are agreed on that.'

Holly heard Carys and her mother talking in the hall downstairs, their voices low so that she couldn't catch the actual words. Moments later, Mum came back into the room with more tea and three biscuits on a plate.

'I've put a chicken casserole in the oven. There was one in the freezer. Nice and nourishing, I thought.' She gave a cut-glass smile.

Holly picked up her phone, holding it so that Mum could see. 'I'm going to phone Veronica.'

'Oh.' Mum clasped her hands together. 'Do you have to do it now, so soon?'

'I do.'

'Do you want me to stay?'

'Would you mind not?'

'Of course not, darling. I'll give you some privacy, and keep Carys downstairs.'

Holly waited until her mother had closed the door quietly behind her, then scrolled to the social worker's number.

★ ★ ★

'All done?' Mum wasn't even pretending to smile now. The look on her face tore Holly's heart in two.

348

'All done.'

'What happens now?'

'Now, you get to meet my daughter — your granddaughter — properly. Here.' She held out the baby. Mum looked at Holly. Holly met her gaze.

'You cancelled the adoption?'

Holly nodded.

'Oh. Oh, love.' Laura gathered the baby into her arms, wetting her tiny face with her own tears as she kissed her.

'Don't, Mum. You'll start me off.'

'When did you change your mind? Today?'

'Not really. As soon as I saw her, I knew I'd already decided I wasn't going to give her up.'

She'd been thinking about this all afternoon. There hadn't been an exact moment, an epiphany. Rather a slowly growing knowledge, a dawning. She had enough love for this child, and more, to make up for everything else. It was all she needed, all she'd ever needed.

'Can I ring Clayton, and Emily, and Gran? Shall I go and tell Carys?' Mum's face was alight. She spun round on her heel in front of the window, hands clasping and unclasping.

Holly laughed. 'Yes, ring them. Tell whoever you want, but not Carys. Let me tell her.'

'Yes.' Laura went to the door. 'I'll send her up.' She turned back, raising a finger. 'I'll go down to Ashdown tomorrow, make sure everything's ready for when you want to go back. I don't trust Carys to do it right.' She laughed.

'Mum?'

'Yes, darling?'

'I'd rather stay at home with you for a while. Is that okay?'

'It's more than okay, you know that.'

Holly heard her mother's squeal of delight as she went downstairs, and smiled to herself.

The baby stirred in her arms. One tiny hand broke free of the blanket. She opened her hyacinth-blue eyes and gazed up at Holly.

'It's you and me now, kid,' Holly said. 'You and me.'

*   *   *

'Isaac wants to know if he can come and see the baby,' Carys said the following morning, after Penny had made her promised visit.

'Of course he can come. He doesn't need to ask.'

'Well maybe, just maybe, Holly, he feels a little bit awkward? After you rejected him, I mean.'

'That's silly. We're still friends.'

Carys had a point, although Holly wasn't about to admit it. Before the baby was born — was that really only yesterday? — Isaac had been keeping his distance. She'd tried to rationalise it as coincidence, the way there was always somewhere he had to be if there was any chance the two of them would be alone for any length of time. He was putting some space between them, that was the truth, and that space felt empty

351

and, yes, lonely at times.

There, she'd admitted it, even if it was only to herself. Lorcan had shaken her confidence when it came to love and relationships — shaken, not destroyed. But it hadn't been all one-sided. She was ashamed of the way she'd behaved, leading Lorcan into thinking they could rekindle their relationship because she'd been so selfish as to want one more hour of passion with him. She'd already known then that his personality was bordering on obsessive. If she and Isaac were to have any sort of chance, he'd have to know the full story. She couldn't begin a relationship based on a lie, even if it was a lie of omission.

It was all academic now, anyway. She'd sent Isaac away, metaphorically speaking. She'd lost her chance. Besides, things were different now. She was a mother; her daughter was her priority. There was no room in her head for anything else.

'Earth to Holly?'

Holly looked up from the sofa where she'd been installed since breakfast that morning, the baby in the Moses basket by her side.

'Sorry, I was miles away. Carys, you do understand why I'm not coming back to the house just yet, don't you? I owe it to Mum to give her some time with the baby after what I've put her through. She shouldn't have to visit every time she wants to see her.'

Carys dropped down onto the floor beside the sofa and stroked the baby's head. 'It's cool. You need your mum at a time like this, anyway. She's over the moon that you're keeping this little one, and so am I.'

Silence fell. Holly was thinking about Carys's lost child. Carys probably was, too. She looked a little sad as she fondled the baby.

'You okay, Carys?'

'Yeah, I'm okay.' She looked up and smiled. A look of understanding passed between them.

The doorbell rang. Carys got up to

see but Mum had got there first.

'Look who's here,' she said, coming into the living room.

Behind her, looking slightly pink in the face, was Neville.

'Hope you don't mind me turning up,' he said, 'but the missus sent these over. Ever so excited she was, when I told her about you and the little 'un.'

He was holding a fistful of jewel-coloured dahlias, the stems wrapped in damp newspaper.

'They're gorgeous. Thank you. That's so kind of her,' Holly said, getting up from the sofa.

'No, no, you sit down.' He held up a broad hand.

Carys took the flowers from him. Laura offered him a cup of tea.

'I mustn't hold you up. Just came to bring the dahlias. The missus grows 'em.'

'Neville's brought a dozen eggs from his farm as well,' Mum said. 'Do have a cup of tea, Neville. We're chain-drinking the stuff.'

'Ah, go on then.'

Prompted by Carys, Neville sat in the armchair, perching right on the edge of the seat. 'Looks like she's settled in nicely.' He nodded towards the baby.

'She has, which is surprising since I hardly know one end of her from the other.' Holly laughed.

'Ah, they know when they're well off. Don't you worry. You'll soon get the hang of it. What you callin' 'er?'

'That's what I've been asking,' Laura said, returning from the kitchen.

'And me,' Carys said.

Holly looked at Neville. 'Your missus. What's her name?'

'She's Daisy. Pretty as one, too. That's what I always say.'

'Daisy.' Holly smiled. 'Daisy it is, then.'

★　　★　　★

Flowers arrived at Spindlewood, enough to fill a florist's shop five times over, and dozens of cards. Daisy

355

received toys, and clothes in every colour, but mainly pink.

'There's more to come,' Carys said, wrinkling up her nose at a candy-pink knitted cardigan. 'Nan's still at it. Valerie must have run out of pink wool by now, surely.'

Valerie was a friend of Mum's; she owned the wool shop in the village.

'I like it,' Holly said. 'It suits her colouring.'

'Not blonde, like you, is she?'

The baby's hair, the little there was of it, was dark, chocolatey brown. The same as Lorcan's.

'She might be, later on. They change all the time.'

'Yeah. I expect they do.'

Holly's grandmother rang to say she'd bored all her friends to distraction with the photos of Daisy that Holly had sent to her phone.

'Come and stay when you're all sorted. The invitation still stands, only now it's for two!'

On the third morning, a basket of

pink and white roses arrived with a teddy-shaped balloon attached to the handle.

A girl! That's cool. Love and kisses, Bethany, Ruomi, Erin and Amber, the card said.

There were visitors as well as gifts. Jo and Lloyd popped in one afternoon after they'd closed the café. Emily came, and of course Clayton. Holly felt a bit guilty. Most likely there were nights he'd normally spend with her mother, but that wouldn't happen while she was installed in her old bedroom. At least, she hoped it wouldn't. She said as much to Carys, who typically made it into a huge joke.

'They've got Clayton's cottage if they want to get it on,' she said.

Mum had come from the kitchen to find out what was so funny, which made them laugh all the harder, until Mum was laughing too, still with no idea what she was laughing at.

The one person who hadn't visited was Isaac. Holly tried not to mind. He worked long hours; the last thing he'd want to do after a hard day at the practice was trek up here to see her. He'd texted his congratulations and sent a card via Carys, some gardenia bath cream for Holly, and a fluffy white rabbit for the baby. Holly had texted her thanks, and added *See you soon?* He'd replied in just one word: *Sure*.

And then, on the fourth morning, there he was. Holly's mother had gone to work leaving strict instructions that she was to ring if there was the slightest problem. Carys was on duty at The Ginger Cat and would be straight up after she finished at two. It was the first time Holly had been entirely alone with Daisy for hours at a stretch; it felt a bit strange.

She'd just fed the baby and was holding her to her shoulder, a muslin underneath, when she heard a car and knew it was him by the sound of the engine. Even so, shockwaves flew up her spine at the sight of him.

'Motherhood suits you,' Isaac

observed when they were in the living room and he'd admired the baby.

'It's a bit early to tell.'

'No, I meant you look great.'

'Thanks.'

'I would've come sooner, only . . . '

'You've been busy, it's fine.'

'Not that busy.'

'Oh, well . . . '

'I'm finding this harder than I'd thought. You. Me.' He shrugged. 'It's okay, you don't need to say anything.'

Holly took Daisy over to the window and laid her in the new buggy, then came back and sat on the sofa next to Isaac.

'My head's in a muddle. I don't know what I think or feel about anything at the moment except the baby.'

'Of course. Like I said, you don't need to say anything. My timing's rotten, as always.'

'There isn't a wrong time for honesty. I should try it more.' She gave a little laugh. Isaac smiled.

'I've taken some time off work, and I'd like to spend some of it with you and your beautiful baby. Make you lunch, just be around in case you need anything. If you'd been at Ashdown, I'd have done the same. No other agenda, hidden or otherwise.'

'I'm not very organised. I'll probably drive you nuts.'

'That's a risk I'll have to take.'

★ ★ ★

Holly felt thoroughly spoiled, and very, very lucky. Carys had come to some arrangement with Jo and Lloyd and freed herself to be at Spindlewood when Laura was at work and Isaac wasn't there. The pair of them were in and out like the figures in a weather-house. Occasionally, they were both there at the same time, neither seeming willing to leave.

'Haven't you had enough of me yet?' Holly asked, half-jokingly, when the three of them were sitting round the kitchen table at eleven one morning, with mugs of hot chocolate and brick-sized slabs of gingerbread sent from the café.

'Yep,' Isaac said. 'She's the draw now.' He thumbed towards the corner of the kitchen where Daisy was asleep in her buggy, and winked at Carys.

'I should come home soon,' Holly said half to herself. 'Back to Ashdown.'

'In your own time, babe,' Carys said. 'No rush, is there?'

The doorbell sounded. Isaac was on his feet immediately. That was something else Holly appreciated. She'd had no idea how many callers Spindlewood could have in a day. She'd be feeding or changing the baby, grabbing a moment to wash her hair or simply to have a ten-minute lie down, when the bell would go again and there'd be a delivery man with a parcel, or somebody selling something, or some kind person from the village 'come to have a peek at the new arrival'. Isaac, in particular, was adept at fending them all off in a sweetly overprotective way.

'Somebody to see you, Holly,' he said, coming back into the kitchen. His face was white. 'He wouldn't say his name, so I told him to wait outside.'

Something clicked inside Holly's brain. Quietly, she got up from the table, walked through to the dining room and peered out of the window. He was standing a little distance from the front door with his back to her, hands in pockets, feet scuffing at the gravel. There was no mistaking him: Lorcan.

She darted back to the kitchen. 'Carys, would you take Daisy upstairs, please.'

Carys was already on her feet. 'Why? What's the matter?' Then, seeing Holly's face, 'Oh my God, it's him, isn't it?'

Isaac looked from one to the other of them, trying to make sense of what was happening. Holly had an idea he was more than halfway there.

'Do you want me to get rid of him?'

'No, Isaac; I need to deal with this. Could you, please . . . ?'

'Stay out of the way? No problem.'

He followed Carys upstairs. He wasn't happy about it, Holly could tell, but there was nothing she could do about that. Taking a deep breath to calm herself, she went along the hallway and opened the front door.

Lorcan swung round. 'Holly!'

He stepped forward. It was all she could do not to step back. And then he smiled, and her stupid heart leapt. What was wrong with her? Hormones again. Baby brain. She forced herself to remember the person he'd turned out to be.

'What are you doing here? How did you find me?'

'It wasn't hard. I couldn't remember the name of the house, but you described it, with the turret and everything. The first person I asked in the village told me where it was.'

'You came all the way from Birmingham? You knew I didn't want any more to do with you. You *knew*, and you still came?'

Holly gave her head a little shake, as if he was an apparition she could make disappear.

'I had to know if it was true, and I reckoned the only way to do that was to come and see you in person. Were you pregnant? Is that why you left university?'

He was staring now, looking her over, searching for clues. She was wearing the dark purple tunic she'd worn in the early days of her pregnancy, over black leggings. She looked pretty normal, she thought. A pity she didn't feel it.

She sighed. 'All right, yes. I was, but I'm not now.'

At least it was the truth.

Lorcan bit his lower lip as he tried to process what she'd said. He was probably thinking she must have lost the baby early on or had a termination. She wasn't about to enlighten him. His eyes were overbright, dancing over her face. Drawn to them, she noticed the scar below his eyebrow, faded but visible in the bright light.

She softened her voice. 'Lorcan, I'm sorry if I made you unhappy, but you have to let this go — let *me* go. I wish I could help you, but I honestly don't know how to, and I really don't know what you're doing here, what you expect from me.'

'A bit of consideration would be nice. The *truth*, Holly. We might have been over, but how could you hide something that important from me?'

How, indeed. Was there no end to this? Just when she'd got everything straightened out in her head, known irrefutably that she'd made the right choices, all the old doubts and anxieties were racing back, falling over themselves to get to the front of the queue.

'Holly, can I come in? We can't talk properly on the doorstep.'

'No, I'm sorry but I can't do this. It's too sudden, too much of a shock.'

'Well, how do you think I felt, finding out you were pregnant with my child?'

'I never said it was anything to do with you, Lorcan. You listened to gossip. You put two and two together and came up with five.'

'I'm not stupid, Holly. Give me some credit.' He put a hand to his head, glancing away, then back. 'Sorry, sorry. I had no intention of saying any of that, blaming you. But I had to know, and I had to see you. Please?'

She could hardly let him come hundreds of miles to be sent away with absolutely nothing; she couldn't be that hard-hearted.

'Are you staying somewhere?'

'Yes, the Travelodge on the road down to the coast. I got a taxi there last night from Lewes station — it cost an arm and a leg — and then I got a bus to the village this morning.'

'Come back tomorrow. In the morning, about ten. We can talk then, when I've had the chance to get my head round this.'

'Okay, thanks. But just tell me this. What happened with the pregnancy?'

Holly didn't have time to formulate an answer; Daisy did it for her. Lorcan's mouth dropped open as the shuddery cry of a newborn floated down from upstairs.

'You had the baby! You actually had the baby.' Lorcan nodded, and then his face broke into a wide, slow smile.

'Tomorrow, Lorcan.'

Holly closed the door. From the dining room window, she watched as he paused at the top of the steps to look back at the house before he walked away, down the drive.

16

Holly couldn't catch her breath. She walked along the hall to the kitchen, hardly seeing where she was going. Her one thought was, thank goodness her mother wasn't in.

At once, Isaac and Carys were there. Carys thrust the baby into her arms and she held her close, kissing her velvety-soft forehead, inhaling her milky-sweet smell.

'It *was* him, wasn't it? Lorcan, the one who fathered her — I won't say her father, not the same thing. The one who was violent with you.'

Holly looked from Carys to Isaac.

'It's okay, he knows all about it. I told him while we were upstairs. Sorry if I shouldn't have.'

'No, it's fine. I'm glad you did.'

It was true, she was glad Isaac knew. Whatever he thought of her now, it was too late to worry.

She dropped into a chair. Daisy squawked. She needed feeding, which was all to the good. Holly wasn't in the right frame of mind to be holding this conversation. She just wanted peace and quiet to think about what had just happened, and where she went from here.

'What the hell did *he* want, coming here?'

Carys's face was ablaze with fury. She circled the kitchen twice, the soles of her trainers slapping the flagstones. Holly had the idea she would have thrown something, had the baby not been in the room. Isaac, conversely, was being very still and quiet.

Holly related the gist of the conversation; there were no secrets left now, nothing to hide. Carys was appalled when she got to the part about Lorcan coming back tomorrow.

'It's fine. I can handle it. Don't worry about me,' Holly said. Then, half to herself, 'I've got a lot of thinking to do between now and then.'

'What about? Surely there's nothing to think about?' Carys picked up a mug from the counter and banged it down again, then glanced at Daisy. 'Sorry. But, Holls, honestly. You should've told him to get the hell outta here and not come back, ever!'

Isaac looked at Holly, then more pointedly at Carys.

'I think you should tell her now. Tell Holly what you told me.'

'Tell me what?' Daisy began crying in earnest. 'I'm going upstairs to feed her. Carys, come up with me if you like.'

★　★　★

Isaac had left the house, leaving Carys to say goodbye for him, and he'd see her tomorrow. Holly listened to his car going down the drive, its engine fading into the distance. Perhaps he wouldn't want anything to do with her now, and who could blame him?

Carys seemed to read her mind. 'He

understood, Holly, he really did, and he was so sad about what had happened to you, what that bastard Lorcan did. He doesn't think badly of you, any more than I do.'

'We'll see.' Holly sighed regretfully, shifted in the low velvet-padded arm-chair, and moved Daisy to the other breast. 'Anyway, I can't think about Isaac now.'

'I know. I was just saying, in case you were wondering. Look, I don't know if you're ready to hear this, but you're going to hear it anyway, just in case you were having any doubts about the other one. Lorcan.' She spat out the name. 'Tell me you aren't going to let him be Daisy's father, after all you said?'

'It's made me think, him coming all the way from Birmingham to find me. It made me think that everyone's allowed to make a mistake — no, let me finish — and some people make terrible mistakes, and pay for them. But does that mean they don't deserve forgiveness? He regrets what he did, he regretted it the moment he did it. Do I have the right to withhold that forgiveness, forever? I don't have feelings for him, not in the same way as before. But I do have compassion.'

'Well then, you *definitely* need to hear this.' Carys pulled her feet up onto Holly's bed and sat cross-legged. 'But first, let me check something with you. Lorcan's surname is Jones, right?'

'Right . . . ?'

'And he comes from the Swansea area?'

'He's from Wales, not sure exactly where. Now you say it, though, I think he did mention Swansea once.'

In the early days, when they'd talked as much as they'd kissed, Holly had told him all about Spindlewood and Charnley Acre. He'd liked hearing about her childhood, but now she thought about it, he'd given very little away about his own home and upbringing.

'Oh, that's where you come from, isn't it? Near Swansea? That's a coincidence.' Daisy detached herself. 'Can you pass me one of those breast pads?'

'Holly, *listen.*'

Did she have to? Hadn't she had enough bad news for one day? She couldn't imagine what Carys had to tell her, but it wasn't going to be good news. It was written all over her face.

'Okay, I'm listening.'

'I recognised him straight away, when I saw him from the window — we were in the turret.'

'You *know* Lorcan?' Holly swallowed.

'I went to secondary school with him. We weren't in the same class, we weren't mates or anything, but I used to see him on the school bus.'

'And?'

'His father used to knock his mother about. I wouldn't have known, only their next-door neighbours worked at our hotel for a while — him as a cellar man and her as a waitress — and they knew all about it. Lorcan's mum cleared off once, but she came back for the boys. She used to say her husband had a temper on him that he couldn't control. Justifying his behaviour. Not right, though.'

'Carys, are you sure this is the same family you're talking about? Half of Wales is called Jones.'

'Totally sure. Sorry, Holly. What I'm trying to say is that that sort of behaviour can be learned, but there's also evidence — scientific evidence — to suggest it can also be genetic. We heard that Lorcan's elder brother punched his girlfriend in the face because he caught her talking to another bloke. I can't say that's the gospel truth, but these rumours don't start from nothing. If Lorcan has that streak in him, it will always be there, unless he does something about it.'

'Carys, I wound him up, not deliberately, but I slept with him when I shouldn't have and then I said 'no'. I gave him mixed messages, and he was still upset about being dumped, and . . . '

'Holly, no! Even if it's in his genes to lash out like that, he is still responsible for his own behaviour. What he did was totally unacceptable. You do see that, don't you? Please tell me you do. You can ask Isaac. He said exactly the same. Lorcan Jones clearly has a problem and that's sad, but it's not *your* problem. Let him have contact with Daisy and you'll never sleep at night.'

Holly looked down at Daisy, now nodding off to sleep in her arms. Her precious little girl. She knew Carys was right; she just didn't want it to be true. Lorcan wouldn't hurt his daughter, she felt certain, but she mustn't ever be a part of that family.

'Thank goodness she's a girl,' Holly said quietly.

'I know.' Carys nodded. 'Something else I wanted to say. It's none of my business, I know, but I think you should tell your mum the whole story about Lorcan. If it was Daisy, you'd want to be put in the picture, wouldn't you?'

'Yes, and I will tell her. Just let me get tomorrow over and then I will.'

★ ★ ★

It wasn't easy, leaving Daisy, but she didn't have any choice, and she'd have a genuine reason for not staying long. Lorcan hadn't been happy about not being invited back to the house — his curt reply to her text signalled that — but this was her call.

At ten minutes to ten, Holly settled Daisy in her buggy with Carys in charge, then got into Isaac's car and they drove down to the village. Isaac waited in the little car park behind the high street and Holly walked the few yards to the stone bench beside the war memorial. Lorcan raised a hand in silent greeting as he made his way over from the other side of the street. He began to speak as soon as he sat down, but Holly held up a hand.

'Me first.'

She kept her speech straight to the

point, without emotion or ambiguity.

'No, that can't be true,' Lorcan said, disbelief written all over his face. 'I can count, Holly, and we got together at the time. I don't know why you're lying to me.'

Oh, how she wished she didn't have to lie! But it was the only way.

'You were quick enough at the time to accuse me of seeing somebody else. You thought it was Stefan, don't you remember? Well, you were half right. I was seeing someone at the time. Not Stefan. It was someone I met at the party at Christmas.'

There was no need to embroider the lie, but a little extra colour might help convince him. She could tell Lorcan was wavering, beginning to think she might be telling the truth.

'Who? What's his name?'

'You don't need to know that. Only that it happened. You've had a wasted journey, Lorcan. I can't go back — we can't go back — and you need to go back to Birmingham and forget about me, leave me to bring up my daughter in the way that's best for her.'

He reached across to put an arm around her shoulder. She shrugged him off, gently.

'Lorcan, please don't make this any harder for yourself. I'm sorry, okay?'

'I wanted to see the baby. I don't care if she isn't mine. I could love her, like I love you, I know I could.' Lorcan's tone smacked of desperation.

Holly bit her lower lip. She wasn't prepared for this, although she shouldn't have been surprised.

'Lorcan, you didn't come here for me, or the baby. You came because you wanted redemption from what you did to me.'

Was that true? She didn't know, but it made sense as the words came out, and judging by the look in Lorcan's eyes, she'd hit the nail on the head.

He let a moment's silence fall, then, 'Do you forgive me, Holly? I am truly sorry.'

'Yes. I forgive you.'

Minutes later, Holly watched Lorcan cross the road and head towards the bus stop before she returned to the car.

'All right?' Isaac said, starting the engine.

'Yes. Thanks.'

Nothing more was said as they drove back to Spindlewood. Isaac glanced at her and smiled a couple of times. Comforting, reassuring.

Her heart swelled with love for him.

17

On Holly's last night at Spindlewood,
two weeks after Daisy's birth, Mum
cooked a special dinner, setting the
table in the dining room. It was just the
three of them: Holly, Mum, and
Clayton. Four, if you counted Daisy,
who obligingly lay quietly in her buggy
until the lemon meringue pie appeared,
by which time she'd obviously decided
she'd had enough of being ignored.
Laura ate her pie while jiggling Daisy
on her lap.

There was champagne; Holly allowed
herself a quarter of a glass. 'What are
we celebrating?'

'Daisy's birth, the pair of you going
home to Ashdown. What else do we
need?' Mum's laugh had something else
behind it.

Clayton rolled his eyes. 'What your
mother's trying to say, without actually

saying it, is that — '

'Oh! You're moving in! And about time, too.'

Holly let out a peal of giggles. The champagne had gone straight to her head; it was the first actual drink she'd had in many months.

'Yes, that. But something else.' Clayton looked at Laura. 'Shall I tell her, or will you?'

'For Pete's sake, you two are like a couple of coy teenagers! Tell me *what*?'

'Hang on.' Laura passed the baby to a surprised Clayton and left the room.

When she came back, she held out her left hand. On the third finger was a slim gold band with three small diamonds in a triangular setting.

'A ring! Mum!'

'Yep. I'm making a decent woman of her,' Clayton said, beaming all over his face.

Holly hadn't expected that, although now she thought about it, it felt right for her mother to be getting married again.

'When is it, the wedding?'

'Oh, we haven't got that far,' Mum said, sitting down again and claiming back the baby. 'We only decided while we were on holiday in the Lake District. We bought the ring there, in a lovely little jeweller's. It's antique.'

Holly laughed again. 'Well, make sure the pair of you aren't antiques by the time you make it down the aisle.'

'Oh, by the way,' Laura said, 'what was it you wanted to talk to me about?'

'It's not important. Not tonight, anyway. It'll keep.' She smiled.

★ ★ ★

There were five pink balloons tethered to the door of Ashdown as Holly and Daisy drew up in Isaac's car the following morning. It was Saturday, but Carys had arranged to have the morning off.

She flung open the door and took the carry-cot from Holly. 'Couldn't have you coming home to no welcome party.'

Holly, her arms full of blankets and bags of clothes, stood in the hallway and looked around. It was good to be back, although where all this stuff she'd accumulated in such a short space of time was going to go she had no idea.

Much of it, including the buggy, ended up in the dining room/office.

'Isaac, you're a star, putting up with all this clutter in your house.' Daisy let out a yell that seemed far too loud to have come from such a tiny baby. 'Not to mention the noise.'

'Don't be daft. I'll get the kettle on.' He headed for the kitchen, a broad smile spreading across his face.

'He's made up, Holls. He couldn't wait for you to get home, the two of you. He was afraid you'd stay at your mum's.'

'Was he? He told you that, did he?'

'Not in so many words. Doesn't make it any less of the truth, though.'

'Well, I'm glad to be home. I love our house, and Daisy will, too. Carys, *thank* you.' Holly flung her arms round her friend. 'I mean it. You've been marvellous, running around after me, and for . . . well, the other stuff.'

She meant Lorcan. Carys knew that. Her dark eyes softened. 'As long as you and Daisy are fine, it's all I care about.'

As they entered the kitchen, their arms were entwined.

'Look at you two,' Isaac said, grinning. 'It's the mutual appreciation society.'

'Yup,' Holly and Carys said together.

★   ★   ★

At midday, Carys went reluctantly to The Ginger Cat and Isaac went to meet a mate at The Goose and Feather. He'd asked Holly first if she didn't mind being left alone. She assured him she'd be fine. Actually, it felt good to have the house to herself for a while — herself and Daisy. Besides, she'd have to get used to that. It was Saturday. Isaac would probably be out tonight, too, as would Carys. She had a date with Nick, the guy from the gym. Apparently it wasn't their first date, either.

'That's fantastic! Why didn't you tell me before?' Holly had asked when Carys had let it slip earlier.

'Because I wanted to see if it worked out before you started getting all excited.'

'And has it worked out?'

Carys had nodded, her dark eyes shining, side flicks bobbing. 'I think it's going to.'

Holly couldn't be more pleased that Carys had taken that step. She was lovely and strong and brave. Good on her for not letting that awful Gareth ruin the future for her.

Holly fed and changed Daisy again. Then, while the baby slept in the buggy, she tidied up a bit more, moving some of the things that had been parked in the dining room to her bedroom, and tucking Daisy's clothes and nappies away in the Chinese chest on the landing. It probably wouldn't get painted now, but its ugliness had acquired a strange sort of appeal, so it didn't matter.

Later, she was standing by the open back door, Daisy in her arms, taking the air and inspecting the garden, when Isaac came back. It had begun to drizzle a bit, but the autumnal air was mild, and the baby was well wrapped up in a pink cellular blanket.

'The grass needs cutting again,' Isaac observed, coming up behind the two of them. 'And those shrubs at the back are meant to be clipped or something. Clayton mentioned it. I might have a go tomorrow, if it's not raining.'

'Isaac,' Holly said, turning round, 'I'm sorry. I haven't been very fair to you.'

His grey eyes were wide. 'Haven't you? I'm not sure I understand what you mean.'

He turned and walked into the kitchen. Holly followed. She laid Daisy back in her buggy, tucking the blanket around her, then put a hand on Isaac's arm so that he turned round to face her.

'I think you do. I've pushed you

away, tried to forget about your feelings for me. I've put everything else — everyone else — first, and that's not right. It's not how it should be, considering . . . '

'Naturally, Daisy's your priority now, and Lorcan turning up threw you a curveball. It's fine, I can live with that.'

'I was going to say, considering the way I feel about you. Tell me it's too late, tell me to go away, and I'll understand.'

Isaac smiled, right into her eyes. 'Please don't go anywhere, Holly Engleby, either of you.' He gathered her into his arms. 'When the time's right, come to me, and I'll be here. That okay with you?'

Holly couldn't speak. The constriction in her throat wouldn't allow it. Instead, she put her arms round Isaac and held him as if she would never let him go.

We do hope that you have enjoyed reading this large print book.

Did you know that all of our titles are available for purchase?

We publish a wide range of high quality large print books including:
Romances, Mysteries, Classics
General Fiction
Non Fiction and Westerns

Special interest titles available in large print are:
The Little Oxford Dictionary
Music Book, Song Book
Hymn Book, Service Book

Also available from us courtesy of Oxford University Press:
Young Readers' Dictionary
(large print edition)
Young Readers' Thesaurus
(large print edition)

For further information or a free brochure, please contact us at:
Ulverscroft Large Print Books Ltd.,
The Green, Bradgate Road, Anstey,
Leicester, LE7 7FU, England.
Tel: (00 44) **0116 236 4325**
Fax: (00 44) **0116 234 0205**

Other titles in the
Linford Romance Library:

COUNTRY DOCTOR

Phyllis Mallett

After years away, newly qualified Doctor Jane Ashford returns to her hometown in Essex to become a partner in her uncle's practice. Family and friends are delighted to see her again, including Steve Denny, whose crush on her has never faded. But then Jane meets local Doctor Philip Carson, both handsome and lonely; and when his touch kindles a desire that's almost painful in its intensity, she knows he's the right man for her. The problem is, Steve doesn't see it that way — and he intends to make it clear . . .

GOLDILOCKS WEDDING

Carol MacLean

Goldie Rayner wants her wedding to James to be perfect, and asks her three best friends to help. But April, Rose and Lily have their own problems: April realises that even very self-sufficient people need others sometimes, Rose must deal with the consequences of a break-in at her flat, and Lily is inundated with kittens from an unknown, and unwelcome, benefactor. And as Goldie and James find their differences rising to the surface when emotions run high, is her ex-boyfriend Bryce really the person she should be turning to?

CHRISTMAS AT SPINDLEWOOD

Zara Thorne

Laura Engleby loves Christmas. Her daughter Holly is due home from university, and preparations are in hand for Laura's Christmas Eve party, a tradition started in her late husband's time, to which most of the residents of Charnley Acre are invited. When Clayton Masters, owner of Green and Fragrant Garden Services, finds himself with nowhere to sell his Christmas trees, Laura doesn't hesitate to let him use her garden. But little does she know that the simple act will unleash a winter storm which threatens the future she'd planned for herself.

A RATIONAL PROPOSAL

Jan Jones

When Verity Bowman's uncle dies, she discovers that she's inherited his fortune — as well as his attorney, Charles Congreve. But there's a catch. Concerned that Verity would be tempted to give herself completely to frivolity, her uncle has stipulated that she must first prove to have spent six months 'in a wholly rational manner'. As Charles oversees the conditions of the will, he realises he's falling in love with Verity — but his social position precludes marriage to a wealthy heiress. Can they find a way to make a life together?

BEYOND THE TOUCH OF TIME

Patricia Keyson

A Victorian locket links four stories together, spanning across decades. An aristocrat falls in love with his maid, and heartbreak lies ahead. During World War Two, best friends Barbara and Doreen experience closeness but also jealousy. A young single mother in the 1960s is given the locket, but traumatic events ensue after she casts it aside. And in the present day, Rachel discovers the locket at a car boot sale and wonders about the past of her new talisman, as well as what kind of future it might bring her.

MORE PRECIOUS THAN DIAMONDS

Jean M. Long

Louise Gresham moved to Whitchurch, Kent almost three months ago following a painful break-up with her fiancé. Good fortune landed her a job at Whitchurch Museum, and it is here where she meets handsome thirty-something Nathaniel Prentice. After assisting Nathaniel with his lectures and accompanying him on visits to see his niece, Louise realises she is developing feelings for him. But the past has made her cautious — should she jump straight into another relationship so soon after getting her heart broken?